The Designated Valentine

Drew Taylor

Taylor Made Publishing

To all the girls who only want the man you love to pursue you...
May God light a fire under his bum to do so or may you find a man
who will!

Trigger Warning

This book contains references to a battle with alcoholism.

Warning

♥

What's In This Book?

If you like to fully experience a book for what it is, then skip this section

TDV IS A FRIENDS to enemies to lovers romantic comedy that showcases the pain of unrequited love and then what happens when said unrequited love starts to requite it... It showcases how a man should lovingly and wholeheartedly pursue a woman (especially if he was the one making the BIG mistakes) and the journey it takes a woman to accept it. This is by no means every single person's story, but it is my story. And it is Karoline and Mason's story.

TDV is spice free. There are, however, plenty of kisses, attraction, and longing stares. Why? Because these two have a past. They aren't strangers ogling one another weirdly. Furthermore, attraction and lustful thoughts are a natural, human thing that we battle. I seek to showcase that while also having my characters learn to take their thoughts captive.

TDV contains drinking as it is essential to the certain character's past and storylines. I always try to showcase not only the evils that alcohol can cause but also the way drinking should be handled appropriately.

TDV is spice-free and written from a Christian perspective. I am a Christian, but I do not write Christian Fiction. I seek to write characters who are flawed and sinful, yet, they recognize their need for Christ and seek forgiveness, repentance, and redemption. I wanted to read a romance where faith wasn't the main storyline, yet the characters were Christian and operated from that worldview...so I wrote it.

Read at your own risk. And I pray you LOVE this story. Please leave a review if you do :)

Chapter One

♥

Karoline - Three Years Ago

ONE OF THESE DAYS, that yellow softball hurtling towards me is going to whizz past my glove and sock me in the face if I don't keep my eye on it instead of watching the world's most handsome man gun it at me. With a resounding pop, it lands in the pocket of my glove in the nick of time.

The way his brown hair swishes as his tall, muscular, tanned body leans into the follow-through of his throw takes a day off my life because of how long my heart stops. Why in the world have I not told the man I'm in love with him yet?

After wiping the sweat from my palm onto my oversized t-shirt, I throw the ball back.

Oh, that's an easy question to answer. Mason Kane is entering his junior year of college at twenty-one, and I'm one month removed from graduating my homeschool program at eighteen. He sees me as another little sister. He'd chuckle with amusement and pat the top of my head if I told him

I loved him and had for several years. "Good one, Vroom," he'd say, using the ridiculous nickname he'd given me. He couldn't call me "Kar," short for Karoline, like every other reasonable human would. He decided on "Vroom" because "Kar" sounds like "car," which if you drive the right one, can go fast, and I'm the fastest girl on Dallas High's softball team as he witnessed for six consecutive seasons.

I never said Mason was the brightest crayon in the box, but he sure is the hottest—a smoldering maroon that burns deep and long.

I've already caught his next throw, and I'm preparing to return it when I tune back into what he's rambling on about.

"She's using me. I'm sure of it," Mason says as the ball I've just lobbed hits his glove. Can I tune back out now? The last thing I want to hear about is Mason's love life with a sophisticated, adult college woman.

But instead, I play the helpful friend-slash-little-sister and give him sound (and selfish) advice. "Then just forget about her, Peppermint." Yeah, I call him Peppermint. Mason… Mace… Pepper spray… Peppermint… Last name Kane… You get what I'm saying?

You can't judge me.

He calls me Vroom for crying out loud.

He releases a dramatic, long-winded sigh, holding the ball in his gloved hand and running his other through his thick, chocolate-colored hair. Mason could be a sweaty sports model in his black athletic shorts with hemlines that rest right above his knees, filled out nicely by thighs that could save lives with the power they hold. The white moisture-wicking shirt he wears fits in all the right ways—tight around his rounded biceps and broad chest while hanging a little loose in the torso where I know from personal experience that a four pack of abs sit. God didn't give him six or eight because He knew Mason had to have some physical flaw. *But was it really a flaw?* My mind laughed. *Heh. Nope.* While he never played sports in high school, it wasn't because he didn't have the talent or skill to. He preferred to spend all his time creating music, which is why he up and left me during the school months to go to Nashville for college.

Mason is phenomenal on a guitar, and let's not forget to mention how angelic his deep, breathy voice sounds when he sings. I have no doubt he will make it big one day. I'm not sure why he hasn't other than he's not actively pursuing a record deal. Or maybe it's because he's too focused on girls and partying seven days of the week.

"Impossible," he finally says. Mason looks at me from across the yard. He's not so far away that I can't see the sheepish grin cross his perfect lips, though. "I think she might be the girl I'm supposed to marry. If she'd let me take her out on a real date instead of only asking me to accompany her when she needs a stand-in man on her arm."

Mason throws the ball back to me, and I catch it with gritted teeth. *No, Mason. In fact, she isn't the woman you're supposed to marry. I am. Can't you see that? You're in college, supposed to be smarter than me, and even I know we are meant to be together. How about asking me on a date, you big oaf?*

Instead of revealing my inner desires, I release a haughty snort. "Her loss." Then I use my missile of an arm (thank you, left-field position) to gun the ball back to him.

He jerks his glove in front of his face out of self-preservation just in time to snag the ball, making an *oof* sound as he tosses his glove off and shakes his hand. "Easy there, Vroom. You trying to take my hand off?"

I casually rotate my right arm and then stretch it across my chest. "Just needed to stretch out the arm. Season ended a month ago and I haven't gotten to let loose in a while."

He laughs with a shake of his head then proceeds to sit down under the magnolia tree that's a few paces behind him. "Count me out then. You're too powerful for me, Karoline."

My heart stutters at the sound of my name spoken in his bass-level voice. How can a twenty-one-year-old sound like he's a grown man? Then again, as I keep my eyes locked on Mason and restrain myself from skipping to sit next to him under the tree, my heart flutters because he is very much *homegrown*. Gone is the boyish roundness to his cheeks. He is becoming all lines: sharp but filled-out angles. He shaves his beard, but I know he is capable of growing one based on pictures he posts when he's away. Every time he returns home from Nashville on break, he seems to have evolved even more into a man.

And he's always got a new girl he's talking about, but that's beside the point. None of them have lasted…

I plop down next to him, silently chastising myself for not being more graceful like one of his college girls would be. Also, I shouldn't sit this close. I reek of sweat. June in Dallas,

Texas, is not to be messed around with. Layers and layers of deodorant are required to survive not smelling like a boys' locker room at all times. It's a smell I only know from softball tournaments where we had to utilize said locker rooms.

I scoot away.

"What? Do I stink?" Mason sniffs his own armpit and scrunches his nose. I spit out a laugh. He may be becoming more of a man, but that doesn't stop the boy I know from showing through his new and improved body every now and then.

"No, but I probably do. Just protecting you from my softball sweat." Mason leans over, one hand planted on the ground to keep him from falling into me. As his face nears mine and our cheeks touch, I stiffen. His proximity has encased me in stone. He sticks his nose in the crook of my neck and sniffs.

Before I can regain mobility in my body and shove him, he pulls away, his eyes closed and a soft hum coming from somewhere deep inside his throat. "You smell like dirt and summer. And I believe there's a hint of lavender."

That would be the layers upon layers of deodorant previously mentioned.

But full stop.

Mason Kane *sniffed* me… and he *liked* it? I'm not making that up, right? The closing of the eyes, the hum… He liked my natural scent. I read an article not long ago mentioning how the right person for you would be drawn to you at a subconscious level due to the pheromones you produce.

My jaw hangs agape as I try to wrap my brain around the fact that my best friend put his nose to my neck and sniffed me. *And he was pleased,* my internal voice reminds me.

Something invades my mouth at that moment, and my gag reflexes are immediately triggered. "Agh." I start coughing and spitting as I move to my knees and place my hands on the ground for steadiness. The heaving and groaning noises are equivalent to the Wicked Witch of the West melting after the water is tossed onto her. My breath escapes me, and I swear I'm about to pass out when a strong hand slaps me on my back a few times and the fly buzzes out of my mouth like it didn't make a vicious attempt on my life.

Groaning and catching my breath, I collapse onto my side before rolling flat onto my back.

Beside me, Mason roars. "That was... attractive."

"A fly broke into my mouth. What was I supposed to do?" I groan again, wishing the fly would have murdered me anyway. It'd be better than facing Mason with this heavy weight of embarrassment crushing my chest, severing my blood flow, and causing my cheeks to flush.

Though, to be fair, I legitly couldn't breathe for a minute there.

I cover my face with my hands. "Why?"

"Broke into your mouth? Interesting word choice, Vroom." Mason continues to laugh, and I'm a bit peeved he hasn't checked on me.

"Well, what else do you call it when something unwanted enters your space?"

"You could have said, 'a fly flew into my mouth.'"

I peek through my fingers to find him sitting next to me, watching me, with a ridiculous smile across his face. *Ugh, I might as well face him.* It's not like embarrassing things haven't happened to me in front of him before. He's my best guy friend, after all.

Sitting up and leaning against the tree, I reply, "I don't like the alliteration or switch of tenses of 'a fly flew'."

Mason's eyebrows knit together, and I'm momentarily consumed by his chocolate eyes that match his perfect, fluffy hair. "You're an odd one."

I shrug, trying my darndest to no longer think about everything that went down in the past few minutes. "Eh, you love me anyway."

Mason's hand approaches my face, and he tilts his head as he tucks a stray lengthy strand of frizzy caramel hair behind my ear. My heart leaps and gallops as his guitar-calloused fingers slide against my cheek, and I'm once again converted to a statue.

"That I do, Vroom. Very much so. You're my best friend."

Chapter Two

♥

Karoline - Present

"THREE, TWO, ONE..." THE world erupts in fire-work-induced explosions as couples around me kiss to ring in the new year. White, gold, blue, red, and purple displays of color fill the sky as "Auld Lang Syne" blasts from the speakers inside Lake View, a local restaurant with rooftop seating that overlooks the catfish farm directly outside city limits in Juniper Grove, Mississippi. It's not the prettiest view in town, but with fireworks popping across the way, it's quite gorgeous compared to most nights. Twinkle lights are situated around the rooftop and all the cafe-style black wired tables and chairs have been removed so people could use the top as a dance floor and firework-viewing area for the night. But at this moment, instead of dancing, everyone is lip-locking, and I'm crossing my arms and making the same face that a two-year-old trying a lemon for the first time would make.

"See? I told you that you'd have fun." Chanel Wright, my closest friend, second cousin, and, for all intents and purposes, my partner in crime, swings one arm around my shoulders while downing the rest of her champagne. Her boyfriend, Malik, takes the glass flute away after she finishes. "The best night of my existence," I deadpan, shifting my weight to relieve the pressure created from my black stiletto booties. Seriously? What part of my facial expression gave her the idea that I was having fun? Was it the pursed lips, the narrowed eyes, or the crossed arms as I stood uncomfortable as everyone sucked face?

Chanel giggles then hiccups, stumbling sideways, dragging me with her.

"That's enough for you, babe," Malik says, snaking an arm around Chanel to steady her as she breaks away from holding on to me. Couples *finally* begin to unglue themselves, giving me the green light to relax. At least Malik and Chanel only engaged in a lingering press of the lips.

Malik turns to me and asks, "Is she going back to your apartment or to her mom's?"

I sigh, shoulders dramatically slumping. Malik offers a sympathetic smile but it evaporates when Chanel takes his cowboy hat off his head, revealing his buzz cut black hair that is only a couple of shades darker than his skin. She plops the hat onto her own head with a party-girl "woo." I scan the area but nobody is paying attention to us. They are still snuggling close with their partners, laughing with friends, and consuming a little too much alcohol. Everyone is joyfully bringing in the new year except me, Little Miss Anti-Romantic. It *would* have been a joyful start to the year if I could have stayed cozied up in my apartment watching the ball drop on the screen while snacking on caramel chocolate popcorn, sipping tea, and sporting fuzzy socks over these stilettos.

"Don't I make your hat look good, babe?" She beams up at her boyfriend, who shakes his head with a flashing smile that says he's over her shenanigans but still finds her to be the most adorable human on the planet.

I hope everyone is still ignoring us. Can't have my cousin getting a reputation. "Okay," I drag the word out. "We gotta get you home. You can't be taking your man's cowboy hat off. Everyone knows what *that* signifies."

Malik laughs but remains gentle with his inebriated girl-friend. "You look better than I do wearing it, that's for sure." He places a soft kiss on her flushed cheek. "But we do need to get you home." He turns back to me. "So, your place or Teresa's?"

"Mine." I groan at the thought of taking care of a drunk Chanel for the rest of the night, but what else are cousins for? "I'll take her with me. You can start your long drive home." Aunt Teresa would kill me for letting Chanel have a couple glasses of champagne. Neither of us drink often, but it's New Year's, and it's our first one celebrating at the legal age of twenty-one, so I let her have her fun. I went into the night knowing I'd be the designated driver, which is fine by me. Personally, I think the Baptists are on to something when they say alcohol is the Devil's drink. That one night three years ago certainly felt like hell…

"Thanks, Kar. I've got to be back on the base by six a.m. It's going to be a long night." Malik works at the airforce base on the coast of Mississippi, which is about a six-hour drive south from Juniper Grove.

I grab Chanel around the waist as Malik pries her hands from around his neck. "I'll miss you," she whines. Malik is unbothered by her girlie cry of affection and leans in to kiss her on her forehead before giving me a hug.

"Bye, my love. Bye, Kar. See you both in a couple of weeks." With that, Malik walks through the double glass doors into the restaurant and disappears into the crowd of people inside.

"Mm, I miss him already." Chanel slumps against me and I stumble sideways in my heels trying to catch my balance. "I'm going to marry him one day."

"Yes, you will, Channel," I say, using her nickname from childhood. It was hard for me to pronounce her name correctly as a little girl, so I called her Channel, and it stuck. "Let's go home before you pass out on me and I have to carry your butt."

"I only had three glasses," she says with a slight slur to her words, but she slings her arm around my shoulders anyway.

"And that's enough for a woman who doesn't drink but maybe once a month." I hold Chanel's waist as we stagger together across the rooftop and down the stairs. While trying to keep her steady, I accidentally bump into a broad chest. I glance up to apologize, but I'm interrupted by Chanel breaking free of my hold. I murmur an apology and scoot around the man, noting his fancy-looking brown Oxford shoes that have a Gatsby-vibe to them, and catch up with my cousin. We make it through the restaurant, which is now playing "New Year's Day" by Taylor Swift, and then we're out the door headed to my lakeshore blue Chevy Malibu.

"Karoline?" A deep, familiar voice catches my attention as I'm opening the driver side door. Searching for the owner of the voice in the midst of the dark parking lot, I see the silhouette of a broad man, and as he steps into the street light, I notice the Gatsby-style shoes. Dragging my eyes up to meet his face, my heart stops. Giving in to the immediate flight response, I throw myself in my car, banging my head against the door frame.

"Karoline! Wait, please!" he shouts, and I glance through my rearview mirror to see the man encroaching my space.

No. He's not supposed to be here. Why is he not at Ole Miss?

Hurriedly, I crank the car and spin out of the parking spot, rocks flying underneath my tires, and, if God is willing to bless me, hopefully pelting the man jogging towards me in his obnoxiously pretty face.

"Whoa," Chanel says, clutching the handle above the door.

Once he and Lake View are out of sight, I finally allow myself to breathe. What in the world is Mason Kane doing here, on my turf, during New Year's Eve?

"Thank you for coming out with me," Chanel says, though my thoughts are not even in the vicinity of receiving her thanks. I nod with a soft smile as I clench the steering wheel, focusing on the feeling of the leather beneath my fingertips.

Chanel pokes me in the arm.

"What is it?"

She clicks on the light in the car. "Seriously. I know you don't do parties much, and I know you still miss him, but thanks for trying tonight. You're going to find someone someday. One day you'll quit loving him. Or maybe he'll surprise you and come back for you. He's changed, you know? Have you seen the interviews where he talks about how he doesn't drink anymore and stuff?"

I stiffen before twisting my head and locking eyes with Chanel for a brief moment. Her hazel eyes are dazed and crescent-mooned, and her short auburn bob is flopping to the side as she tilts her head. She obviously didn't see him before I flew out of there on two wheels, so why does she think he'll be coming back for me? Pressing my lips into a firm line, I say, "I'm fine."

"You're not, but okay," she says before leaning back in her seat and closing her eyes. Why do drunk people always speak nonsense?

The drive back to my apartment is only fifteen minutes, but that gives me plenty of unwanted thinking time. Regardless of what I said, I'm most obviously not fine. Chanel is right in her drunken observation, even if I don't want her to be. It's not like I'm choosing to emotionally react this way. I want to move on, but it's impossible when the man who broke me is on billboards, his voice cascades through radio waves, edited fan videos circulate social media on the regular, and the entire female population is obsessed with him.

Not to mention showing up in flesh and bone to personally ruin any semblance of fun I had at the New Year's party.

This is the second time he's shown up, taking me off guard. Seeing him in person at my boss's wedding a couple of weeks ago shook me to my core. Prior to that, I truly was fine.

For the most part.

I mean, it had been three years since I last spoke with Mason Kane (I can't say it's been three years since I've last seen him because there was that one erratic, hair-brained moment a year ago…). I had even gone on a few dates and had my first real kiss, but nothing stuck. See? I'm *fine.*

But then Mason had the nerve to sing at Hadley and Braxton's wedding, which I'm still unsure as to how that happened or how the two know him. I didn't have the guts or willpower to ask Hadley about it at the wedding just in case my sour expression worried her on her special day, and I haven't seen her the past two weeks since she has been on her honeymoon, leaving the responsibility of managing Southern Grace Boutique and Gift Market in my hands for the time being.

I thought maybe he left after the wedding, going back to Dallas or Nashville or wherever it was he was getting his kicks these days. I knew he was in Oxford for New Year's Eve, but that's an hour away and is supposed to still be going on. Seeing him by happenstance lately was like a knife to the heart. No, that's too cliché. It was like stepping in cow patties while playing hide and seek in a field in the dark. It was like having salt poured into your tea rather than sugar. It was like stubbing your pinky toe on the corner of your bedpost in the middle of the night. Seeing Mason Kane was uncomfortable at best and excruciating at worst.

I whip into the small two-story complex, waving at Lucy Spence as she glances over her shoulder while walking up the stairs to her apartment. The glow of the lights illuminates her strawberry blonde hair and pale, freckled face, and the way she sniffles through a saddened smile tells me she's been crying. I'll have to text her in the morning to check in. She lives in the apartment directly above me with her twin sister, Lorelei, and also happens to be one of Hadley's best friends. Since moving into the place a week before Hadley's wedding, I've gotten to know the twins well. Turns out they went to the same college—Juniper Grove University—where I'm going to be starting my last semester next week. They are four years older than me, though, so I started school after they graduated.

Which makes them only a year older than Mason.

Ugh. How long will it be before my brain stops connecting everything back to him? Seeing him tonight, knowing he's in my town right now…

Well, I think the process of moving on and forgetting about my painful unrequited love will have to start over.

"We're home. Let's go," I bark at my cousin while giving her a harder-than-needed shake. She mumbles and stirs but doesn't open her eyes. "Come on, Chanel. Let's get inside and then you can sleep your life away."

She still doesn't budge, so I get out, slam my door closed (and feel a tad guilty for taking my anger out on my car), then walk to the passenger side to drag Chanel out of the car.

It works, and she stumbles after me as we make our way to the apartment, 108, which thankfully, does not involve stairs like the restaurant did.

I reach for my keys somewhere inside my little black Kate Spade crossbody purse, find them, then unlock the door.

Chanel immediately crashes on the couch, and even though I'm frustrated with her, I take her heels off and cover her with a blanket. I know she has my best interests at heart, and I also know she wants to see me move on with my life, but she doesn't understand just how much of a hold that man has had on my heart since I was a teenager.

I've never made it past the first few dates with a guy…

I've only kissed a man who wasn't Mason once…

I've blocked my heart to the possibility of someone loving me and me loving them…

All because my heart has belonged to Mason Jonathan Kane since I can remember, and he ripped it piece by piece with each day that passed when he didn't call or text after he left me sitting in a corner booth at Dallas Junction diner to turn into an ancient relic of his past and collect dust.

Chanel wasn't too far off the mark when she said I still loved him, and if I've learned one thing about people, it's that when they drink, they say what they really mean and speak to how they really feel.

Chapter Three

♥

Mason - Present

I CHOOSE A TABLE near the wall constructed of pristine windows in Books and Beans and sit down in the seat directly facing the afternoon sun (it's the perfect excuse to keep my sunglasses on while indoors). The small coffee shop-slash-bookstore isn't crowded, but when your name is as big as mine, you always have to err on the side of caution and security. The press knew I was in Mississippi a couple nights ago to perform as part of a New Year's Eve lineup hosted at Ole Miss (which I should have just stayed at instead of ditching the rest of the performances to try and track down Karoline before the clock hit midnight on a delusional notion that she'd throw her arms around me and kiss me senseless in the name of missing me). But back to the press, they didn't know I was hanging around Juniper Grove, as I have been the past few weeks. And thankfully, the owner of this place has instructed her employees not to alert anyone to my presence when I sneak in to visit. I have been hiding pretty well, if I do say so myself.

Speaking of, my security guard, who I typically like to evade, sits a few tables over, sipping the caramel vanilla latte he ordered moments ago. It was a fascinating thing watching a deadly sniper man (retired Marine) sip a sugary latte. A middle-aged woman with a child inside a stroller stands in line behind a short, gray-haired man at the wooden counter to order while two teenage girls whisper and giggle in the middle of one of the five book stacks on the other side of the building. The café specials, which are New Year's related since it's only the second of January, are on display, written in artistic fonts on a chalkboard by the bakery items. There are no overhead lights in the building, typical of coffee shops these days, so the space is illuminated only by the sunlight filtering in through the five window panels making up the half of the storefront I'm sitting in, the dimmed lights strung across the ceiling, and a few lamps stationed in darker corners where the sunlight does not reach to banish the shadows. All in all, it's a calming space with its chestnut wooden furniture, plant life, and earthy tones.

"Fancy seeing you here," a deep voice with the signature Mississippi twang says from behind me. I twist around to see Braxton Rawls, a tall, burly man with dark brown hair and the scruffy start to a beard. If we were animals, he would be a grizzly bear and I'd be a black bear. (Don't ask me why I think of people as animals. It's something I've done for years.)

I met him in a hotel gym in North Carolina a couple months ago. We instantly clicked, partly because he didn't recognize who I was to begin with and didn't go all fan-boy until a few minutes into our short conversation. Furthermore, he had found himself resonating all too well with my viral song "Boyfriend Without Benefits." Even though I wish I never had to sing that song again, I'm thankful it allowed me to meet Braxton, who has an amazing contractor as a brother-in-law.

Braxton also happened to live in the same town as the love of my life, but that's a moot point as I've learned over the past two weeks that Karoline Wright hates my guts.

As he sits down in the chair to my left, the door opens and in walks my current roommate, Finley Andersson, a tall, slender man with blond, shaggy hair. The cool thing about Finley? He's a prince to a little island country called Korsa located south of Norway. You get to meet pretty cool people being as famous as I am, but I'll admit, Finley is the first member of royalty I've met.

"Hey, guys," I nod once to the both of them as Finley sits to my right. "What are y'all doing here at this time of day?" It is past the morning coffee rush, but not quite brunch time yet, which is why I like to stop in around this time during the weekdays.

"I was going to grab a coffee for the wife and run it by the store to surprise her before heading out to work on your house," Braxton says. "She was complaining this morning that she only had decaf at the store and didn't have time to make a coffee run."

Finley jumps in. "I was taking a casual morning stroll down main street when I saw Braxton enter and you sitting here." He shrugs. "I didn't want to be left out, so I joined."

The barista comes to our table and takes our coffee orders—Braxton and I get black drip coffee while Finley orders a fancy-sounding macchiato with special flavoring and milk requests. She delivers the drip coffee in a matter of minutes then goes back to work on Finley's multi-part order.

"It's freeing being in such a small town in Mississippi." Finley grins and leans back in his chair, tossing his hands behind his head in a casual display. "I don't have to wear sunglasses indoors or style my hair differently." He reaches over and ruffles the top of my head, which causes some of my thick, neck-length hair to pull from its ponytail holder in its half-up position.

I swat his hand away and gather half my hair to put back into a mid-bun. "Jeez, man. Cut that out." I don't typically put my hair in a ponytail holder; it's usually left to flow freely, but since I'm trying to be inconspicuous, I styled it differently.

Braxton coos, "Awe, you're such a pretty man." Thankfully, he keeps his hands to himself. He's not as touchy-feely as Finley is.

I scowl, but Braxton continues to speak, shifting his attention to Finley while I finish tying off my hair. "You're going back to Korsa at the end of the week, though, right? 'Cause that's what I told Hadley. You know she wants to set you up with Lucy as quickly as possible."

The waitress brings Finley's drink. He takes a sip and makes a pleased humming sound. He wiggles his eyebrows after setting his drink down. "Indeed. I'm anxiously awaiting our first date when I return from Korsa in a couple of months."

"Careful, Prince of Hearts. You're going to live up to your bad reputation." I pat his back, and now it's his turn to scowl. Finley and I get along well, but teasing each other seems to be our go-to method of showing any sort of affection. We've lived together in Braxton's old semi-secluded cabin for a couple weeks now, but the brotherhood between us solidified quickly as we both understand national pressures of being scrutinized constantly under a spotlight. Him even more so than me, to be honest.

Braxton takes a sip of coffee then says, "Oh, thanks again, man, for agreeing to join Hadley's marketing campaign. That's all she could talk about on the honeymoon. She's stoked to finally connect her jewelry brand to her store."

"Yeah, it's no problem. I'm excited to help y'all out." The black coffee has a toasted taste to it, which is pleasing and reminiscent of autumn.

"Are we still having the previously planned Meatball Monday night at the cabin?" Braxton asks, though mid-way through his sentence, he yawns, distorting the last few words.

"It seems as if someone had a long night." Finley smirks and I raise my eyebrows at Braxton. He returned home from his honeymoon in North Carolina with his long-term best friend and now wife, Hadley, yesterday.

He doesn't even try to hide his wide, toothy grin. He tilts his chin up as he says, "Of course I had a long night. I've had long nights for two weeks. Jealous much?"

"Long nights talking about her work." Finley laughs and I join in, but when Braxton utters something to the effect of "let me tell you about how non-verbal we were," I interrupt.

"Fair enough." I throw my hands up to steer conversation away from his night-time activities with his wife. "How is Michael coming along with drafting the plans for the vacation home?"

Braxton pushes the sleeves of his flannel shirt up and rests his forearms on the table, folding his hands. "We've hit a snag in the design," he begins, and while I listen to the issues they're having and Finley stares at his phone with a wrinkle forming in the middle of his brows—I'll ask him about that later—I vaguely hear the bells ring above the doorway.

Stopping mid-sentence, Braxton waves to someone behind me and says a simple greeting.

"Hey, Braxton. How are you?"

That voice. It sounds familiar, like thick honey and daisies bending under a spring breeze.

"Doing good, Karoline. And yourself? Hadley's not working you too hard now that she's back, is she?"

Oh, no.

The two continue to talk, but I slide a few levels lower into my seat, pressing my sunglasses to my face and tucking my head down. Finley's smirking as if he's watching me simply trying to hide from a fan, but that's not it at all. If the way Karoline peeled out of the parking lot slinging rocks at my face a couple nights ago at the sight of me is any indication as to her opinions towards me, I'm in boiling hot water right now. I've got to continue to keep a low profile until I figure out a rational way to approach—

"Have you met Mason and Finley?" Braxton asks, and I curse under my breath. That's what I get for not sharing vital, personal information with the two guys I can actually chat with in this town as of right now—information that would have stopped Braxton from introducing me at this moment.

He leans over and says, "Don't worry. She's trustworthy. You'll see her around as she works alongside my wife." As if that's my biggest concern right now.

No, my concern is that Karoline Renee Wright, my child-hood next-door neighbor and best friend is standing behind me. I'm concerned not only because of her reaction to me the other night but also because I broke her heart three years ago when she confessed to me, and I did and said unspeakable things in return.

I broke Karoline that night, and though I'm delusional enough to believe she may hear me out and give me a chance, the truth of the matter is that it's a lost cause. Not after what I did and the way I left. But I never touched alcohol again and started to take my faith seriously, adopting it as my own instead of what the church, Dad, and my step-mom told me to believe. So I guess something good came from all the nasty, right?

I'm sure Karoline has moved on, anyhow. Though I reli-giously lurk her socials and there's been no sign of a man, she could just be the type to keep her love life on the down-low.

"I believe I met you at the wedding, Finley," Karoline says. I can feel when her eyes land on the back of my head. "Mason? Hm. You've got an unfortunate name. It's one name I can't stand."

She has to know it's me by the way a seething hiss underlies her words. She wouldn't address a stranger that way. She wouldn't address anyone in that tone…

Except me. Her personal villain.

Braxton and Finley laugh, and I shrink further into my seat. The water I'm in is getting hotter and hotter. If I was an egg, I'd be splitting cracks right about now.

"Careful, Karoline." Braxton chuckles then waves a hand towards me. "You're talking to a famous country singer." I keep my eyes glued to the tabletop as footsteps move from behind me and make their way to the only empty seat at the table—the chair directly in front of me.

"Mason Kane?" she inflects. Her voice, though a more mature sound than at eighteen, is still sweet as honey, but I can hear the poison tones underneath that are reserved just for me.

"Don't act like a stuck-up superstar, Mason. Use your manners and say hello to the lady." Finley shoves my arm. Slowly, I sit up straight in my chair and brace myself for whatever danger awaits me.

I reach for my sunglasses, trying to muster as much of an "I'm an idiot, please forgive me" style apologetic expression as I can.

Blue eyes that mirror violent tidepools burn holes into me. Karoline crosses her arms in front of her and leans towards me across the table, her arms resting on the surface. For all the angry-girl energy she's radiating, and rightfully so, she's stunning. Her light brown hair falls in wavy locks down her shoulders, landing at the edge of the table, and I'm delightfully surprised to see she has bangs. I didn't notice that while rocks ingrained themselves in my skin the other night.

Mercy. Bangs suit her heart-shaped face nicely.

"Oh my goodness! Mason Kane. It's so nice to meet you. I'm a huge fan. I really love 'Midnight Mistakes.' It's my favorite song of yours," she finally says, a bit too loudly for my liking, sarcasm leaking through a gritted smile.

The table falls silent as Karoline and I engage in the scariest battle of don't blink I've ever had the displeasure of being a part of. It's not a game as much as I'm simply too scared to blink in case she launches herself at me. I'm positive her lack of blinking is out of pure spite and serves to make her look like a frightening goddess about to smite me down.

If she really heard 'Midnight Mistakes,' then shouldn't she understand just how sorry I am for what I did to her? The lyrics were a very painful, very public apology that only she would get.

"It's, uh, been a while, Vroom," I stutter over my words, using her old nickname to try and remind her that we were best friends once upon a time.

"I guess it has been, Peppermint," she spits out. Gone is the teasing tone she used to use when she called me that. It sounds like she's damning me to hell as she uses my old nickname.

"Did she say Mason Kane?" someone whispers from behind me, and my attention is yanked away from Karoline's malicious eyes. I place my sunglasses on, stand up, and say, "Well, it's been good, boys. See y'all tonight for Meatball Monday."

I turn my head towards Karoline who has not taken her eyes off me. "Karoline." I nod towards her. "Let's catch up soon?"

She breathes a laugh laced with disbelief and disdain before shaking her head. *Yeah, that's what I thought.*

I speed walk away from the table and towards the door. As I reach for the door handle, I hear Karoline click her tongue and say, "The sheer audacity of that man."

I slip out of Books and Beans, my security guard, careful to keep distance between us so as to not look suspicious, follows me after I get through the door. After I've walked a few blocks to where I parked my truck, I scamper into the lifted black Toyota Tundra and finally allow myself to breathe.

I can handle getting noticed for being Mason Kane, country music superstar, but I can't handle the unadulterated hate burning in Karoline's eyes, especially knowing I'm the fool who put it there.

Seems like three years isn't enough time for some sins to be forgiven.

Chapter Four

♥

Mason - Three Years Ago

L YRICS RACE THROUGH MY mind as I think about my little situationship with Cassidy. We met the first week of classes at college three years ago and have been friends ever since. She's into music like I am and is breathtakingly pretty with her platinum blonde hair and light blue eyes. She flirts with me and asks me to accompany her to events and get-togethers, but she's never taken the next step with me, and when I try to bring it up, she shuts me down and changes the subject.

She has to be into me. That's the only explanation as to why I'm always her stand-in date, right? Maybe she's shy underneath all her extroverted layers? Maybe she likes the man to embark on a chase for a while?

"Hey, Vroom?" I jot down words in my songbook while Karoline sits next to me staring at a blank canvas in the shade of our favorite magnolia tree in her parents' backyard.

"Hm?"

"What does it mean when a girl always asks you to go places with her and do things with her, but she avoids having a define-the-relationship conversation?"

"This again?" Karoline sighs. "Didn't I tell you last week to move on and forget about her when we were throwing the ball around?"

I'm just a boyfriend without the benefits, your favorite arm candy without sweet kisses. The lyrics are flowing, but I have to admit, they are painful. "Yes, but I can't forget about her. She asked me to accompany her to a Morgan Wallen concert in Nashville for the fourth of July, and I want to go, but it's a lot of gas money and time to drive up there for the weekend just to get shut down again. I'm trying to figure out if it's even worth the effort."

"Morgan Wallen is worth the effort alone," Karoline says. I cut my eyes to where she sits beside me, and she wiggles her eyebrows, the paintbrush in her hand momentarily suspended in the air while a still blank canvas sits in her lap. "You can bring me along. I'll help with gas money to see Morgan Wallen."

"Very funny, Vroom. With what money?"

"The graduation money I received, duh."

"You need that money for college, dipstick." I pluck grass from beside me and flick it in her face. A piece lands in her mouth and she starts spitting and using her tongue to get it off her lips. Some kind of built-in warning alarm in my brain begins to blare as I watch her tongue roam the top of her lip, and I get the fiery urge to bite the bottom lip.

Whoa. What in the—

"Forget college. Morgan Wallen is more important. Let me tell you why…"

I shake my head, trying to focus on her words over the intense pounding of my heart and the fog of confusion wrapping around my brain. Did I momentarily find Karoline Wright attractive?

Sure, she's objectively pretty. Any person would have to be blind not to notice, but that feeling was… something else. My body is hot, but I know it's not from the scorching June heat this time around. My eyes are still locked onto her moving lips, and I want to say "to heck with it all" and give in to this animalistic urge to devour her.

But no.

She's Karoline.

"Earth to Mason. Do I have paint on my face or something? What's with that look?" Karoline wipes at her face, and I shake my head clear again, snapping to attention. The momentary lapse in sound judgment is now buried, never to be resurrected again. It's the most obvious thing in the world that Karoline has a crush on me, and while I do tease her occasionally, I can't allow myself to ever intentionally lead her on when I have zero plans to date her. She's my best friend, like a little sister to me, and I don't ever want to hurt her.

"What?" I look away from her intense stare and fiddle with the pen in my hand, smearing black ink against my ring finger. "Oh, nothing. Trying to think about what to do," I say, lying through my teeth. When I turn to Karoline again, she's eyeing me suspiciously with her brows furrowed.

She lets out a breath then returns to her blank canvas as she says, "Okay, Peppermint. Whatever you say. Anyways, I still vote that you let her go. You don't need a girl who keeps you on standby and only asks you out when it's convenient for her."

I mull her words over while doodling on a blank page in my book. As more lyrics begin to surface to finish out the chorus, I fear Karoline may be right. I don't want to admit it because, well, frankly speaking, it wounds my pride and ego. *But I'll come runnin' every time you call 'cause no matter how deep I fall, I'll stay by your side with wounded pride as your boyfriend… without the benefits.*

That's the truth of it, though. My lyrics don't lie. As long as there's a thin, singular strand of hope that Cassidy will accept me one day, I can't let go.

"I'm going to try one more time. If she rejects me at the concert, then I'll call off my pursuit."

I can practically hear Karoline rolling her eyes beside me, but to my surprise she doesn't reply with her usual snark. Instead, she makes a noise that sounds like a grunt and a sigh rolled into one. I risk a peek over my shoulder to where she rests against the magnolia tree beside me. She's zoned in on her painting. I can't quite tell what it is yet, but knowing her, it'll be a sight to behold once it's finished. She has orange paint covering the entire canvas, something she likes to do because, one, it's easier than looking at a blank, white canvas, and two, it gives her paintings a warm glow at the end. Hues of brown at the base of the painting suggest she's doing another autumn landscape, but you can never be too certain with her. She has all kinds of tricks up her sleeve when it comes to her painting process. As I watch her brush strokes, I find my eyes wandering up her arm and to her face. She does, in fact, have orange paint streaked across her cheek and a hint of a smile playing at her lips.

Karoline Wright is objectively pretty, and she is obviously no longer the fourteen year-old-girl who used to follow me around. I guess my body decided to recognize that fact by the way I craved to taste her moments ago. It's amazing what the span of four years can change within a person—physically and emotionally.

As I adjust my seated position, an ache spreads through my shoulder blade from where I fell on it last night after getting a little too drunk with the boys and we broke out into a wrestling match.

That's why I will strangle and stomp out any hints of attraction to Karoline bubbling to the surface. I know my place, and it's not destroying one of the few good things I have in this life. Karoline will meet a nice man from a good family who will protect her and love her and support her. She doesn't need me and my hot mess of a life to drag her down. Karoline is not the type of girl to go out and drink and party with me, and right now, that's what I need in my life: levity and freedom. One day I'll stop, but I'm twenty-one and just want to have some fun. Growing up with my military dad was suffocating, especially after Mom died during my eighth grade year. Yeah, Dad got remarried to a pretty cool woman, but she's not my mom nor has she tried to be since I was already grown at eighteen when they got married.

No matter what, whether I'm into Karoline like that or not, which is undetermined at the moment, I could never be with her. Not until I could be enough for her.

I'm just a hot-blooded male appreciating the beauty of a woman.

And I'm probably just lonely.

Yeah, that's it.

Cassidy will fix it all…

Chapter Five

♥

Karoline - Present

"STUPID MEN. STUPID COUNTRY singers. Stupid flowy hair," I rant underneath my breath, shoving the doors to the store open. I stomp my way through the Southern Grace Boutique and Gift Market, a little too frustrated and a lot too high on thoughts of punching Mason Kane in the face to care about the customers staring at me with open mouths as I trample by. "No Body, No Crime" by Taylor Swift featuring HAIM plays in the background, providing the perfect background music to my mood. I know I should be more like Elsa and "Let it Go," but three years worth of resentment is *impossible* to release in a moment.

I sweep past the racks of clothes, which are hung by color then style, past the now-empty Christmas tree display of candles and locally-made soaps, and finally past the boxes of shoes against the back wall with lingerie tucked in the corner before I barrel into the employee room and slam the once-open door behind me. Hadley stands at the coffee pot, mid-pour into her mug with Dolly Parton's face on it that reads "Best Boss Ever." It's the one I promised her for Christmas before she left for her road trip back in October.

"Delaney is at the register, so we're good to sit in here for a minute. I'm not going to ask if you're fine, 'cause you're clearly not, so how about you tell me what's got you hot and bothered?" Hadley sets the pot down and mixes in sugar and cream while I plop down into the cushioned rolling chair at her desk and bury my face into my hands.

I'm glad you asked, Hads. "Why is he back here casually sitting in my favorite cafe? I thought he left after the wedding? And besides, why *was* he at your wedding? Do you know him or something?"

Heeled footsteps clack from behind me. "Honey, you're going to have to be a little more specific as to who 'he' is." Hadley sits down on the stool I normally sit on when we conference back here. Guilt pricks my conscience because I know my words sound accusing and harsh, but I can't seem to stop. The rant has begun...

"Ugh. I don't even want to say his name... but Mason Kane." His name is as unpleasant as Pop Rocks on the tongue. I lift my head from my hands and twist the chair so I'm facing Hadley. She casually sips her coffee while I'm slowly becoming consumed by a raging hatred as if I'm Hades boasting a hot blue flame of hair for the world to see.

"Ah. Well, he was at my wedding because he, oddly enough, befriended my husband in a hotel gym while we went on that road trip back in October, you know, before we became a thing and all." She takes a sip of her coffee.

"He said he wanted to build a vacation home here in Juniper Grove, and Michael—"

"HE WHAT?!" I rocket to my feet, clenching my fists at my sides. If I were a cartoon, steam would be rising from my head, my face growing redder inch by inch until I look like an overly-ripened tomato.

Hadley's light blue eyes widen to the size of saucers, and my insides sink as regret fills me for lashing out in my anger.

"Okay," she draws out the word, "before I continue, we need to talk about where this fury is stemming from."

"Mason. Freaking. Kane." I grind my teeth, clamping down on my jaw until my back teeth throb with pain. As badly as I feel about lashing out in anger, I can't manage to stop it. It won't go away. Red seems to be the only color I can see right now. "We grew up together. Neighbors."

"Ah, I see." Hadley takes another sip of coffee, a red lip mark lining the rim of the white mug. "And were y'all friendly?"

I sit back down in the seat, crossing a leg and tapping my fingers against the metal desk as I look anywhere but at Hadley. She's going to see right through me in an instant. "Yes. Best friends, in fact."

"Hm. Say no more."

Yeah, I knew I wouldn't have to tell her that I was in love with him. She was in love with her best friend for years. She knows the signs, how that type of thing goes.

"Why is he here? Why did he show up at Lake View Restaurant when he was supposed to be an hour away in Oxford? Why did he want a vacation home here? In this city? There are so many other places in Mississippi he could have chosen if he needed one in this state so desperately." I run a hand through my light brown tresses before making desperate eye contact with my boss again.

Please have the answers, Hadley.

"Well, I'm not entirely sure. He told Braxton that this was the spot he wanted without much of an explanation, and Braxton got Michael hired on to be Mason's contractor. He's been staying in Braxton's old cabin with my college friend, Finley, since the wedding back in December. All I know is that he's sticking around because he wanted to be hands-on during the building process."

I don't respond, thinking through everything she's telling me. Why is he staying here? Shouldn't he be touring or something? No. His tour ended in late November. Not that I should know that. But if that's the case, wouldn't he want to go home to Dallas for Christmas? Why spend it alone here when he could be with his dad, Greg, and step-mom, Jessie? I talked to her just the other day to thank her for the care package she and Greg sent me, and she never mentioned he was here, though she must have known…

Ugh. I wish I could make my brain forget things about him. I wish I didn't check his social media accounts on the regular. *Keep your friends close and your enemies closer,* I tell myself. *Yeah. Right. That's* totally *why I stalk his socials…*

"But if I'm being honest, knowing that the two of you were once besties, and well, it seems like there might have been more there, maybe he's here to reconnect with you, Karoline."

I give Hadley a bombastic side-eye as she shrugs her shoulders and takes another nonchalant sip of coffee. Talking with her has calmed my anger, but my thoughts are still a tornado of questions. Why has he been around for two weeks and not bothered to reach out if he was here to reconnect?

Unless his feeble attempt to catch me on my way out of Lake View on New Year's Eve was his way of reaching? I mean, what did he think I would do? Throw caution to the wind, jump into his strong, bulky arms while his luscious hair blew in the slight breeze? Did he think I would press my lips to his full, plump…

New train of thought, Karoline!
That's right. He's a jerk. A no-good, very bad boy-man.

I finally answer Hadley. "There's no way. You don't know what went down between us… how he left me."

"Do you want to talk about it?"

With a huff, the remaining anger and tension evaporates, replaced with emotional and physical fatigue. "No. I think… well, it hurts too much to talk about."

"Sometimes we need to tell the story to let the pain out. The longer you hold on, the more it will hurt, hun. Healing can begin when you learn to confide in the people who love you. Trust me on that."

Hadley's words make sense, but I don't think I'm ready. Besides Mama, only Chanel knows what he did, and it took a whole calendar year before I told her the story. "One day, Boss. But for now, can you give me a complex task to distract me? Something like rearranging the entire store? Christmas is over, after all."

"Of course. But Karoline, as you know, your internship starts today, and I already had the project for you to complete planned out before I knew everything with Mason…"

The anger that had evaporated begins to rear its ugly head again, but I bite my tongue to keep from reacting. A feeling of dread settles upon my chest at the sorrowful tilt of her head and the way her eyes plead with me to understand.

Through my teeth, I question, "What is it?"

"Valentine's Day is coming up, and you know it's a big deal for our store. This year, I wanted to reveal that Tease Jewelry is associated with our store and start considering branching out the Southern Grace brand across the state and into other southern states, maybe nationally. But to do that, I need bigger publicity. And Mason has agreed, alongside his friend, country music star Genevieve Rhodes, to promote the jewelry and store brand." Hadley pauses, seemingly checking me out to make sure I'm okay. She doesn't know I'm holding my breath and suppressing tears as I nod along to her no good, awful, horrendous plan.

One. I hate Valentine's Day. Two. I hate Mason Kane. Three. I loathe the two of them together entirely.

And Genevieve? I've seen the pictures of her and Mason holding hands, laughing, whispering in each others' ears. Just friends? *Ha. As if.*

"Hadley," I whine in desperation. "Anything else. Really. I'll do anything else."

I'll design a new website. I'll go knee-deep in social media analytics. I'll be the reply girl for emails. All the things that make

me want to pull my hair out because they don't involve working
with actual people. My extroverted soul would go stir-crazy.

"This marketing could give us the support and funds we
need to branch out because of the online orders we will
receive. I've already started back-stocking our most popular
items, but I'll need to focus on the orders and functioning
of the store. I want you to head the marketing campaign,
and it will serve as your internship project hours for the
semester. I'll be reporting directly back to your advisor at
school on your progress. Trust me. You want this project on
your record at school. It's going to be epic, and your name
will be attached to it."

To my emotional demise, she's not wrong. This *is* the
perfect opportunity.

A few seconds tick by before I finally say, "So I'm heading
up the Valentine's Day marketing campaign, and I'll be
working with Genevieve, and," I swallow the bile rising in
my throat, "Mason?"

Hadley nods her head, a sympathetic smile stretching
across her face. She tucks a strand of platinum blonde hair
behind her ear. "I'm sorry, Karoline. I thought you'd be
thrilled to work with the two of them, but I didn't know
your history."

"It's okay. You didn't know. And even so, I have a job to do.
You know I love this place with my whole heart and want
to stay on even after I graduate. I'll do what needs to be done
and won't let my past get in the way. Promise." Oh, I pray
I'm able to keep that promise...

Hadley hops off the stool, and I stand to follow her out onto the sales floor. "I'm so happy to hear that." She stops me before she opens the door to the storefront. "Go wash your face and sip some tea before you come out here. Take some moments, okay?"

I tuck my chin to my chest. "Will do."

"Oh, hello, my sexy husband," Hadley whistles as she steps into the storefront. "You got me coffee? Oh, this is why I love you. I was consuming wretched decaf as quickly as I could in the back of the store."

I can't bring myself to laugh at Hadley's flamboyance as I usually do as I walk to the bathroom. I bet I've looked like a raccoon this whole time. When I make it to the bathroom, the mirror reflects frizzy, long hair, blackened eyes, and a puffy, red face. The image of a girl having to confront the demons of her past.

Excuse me. Demon. Singular.

Getting to work cleaning up my face, I shudder at the thought of what I have to do. Valentine's Day? Really? Working at a boutique, it's no surprise that I would have to market the holiday, but now I have to market it using the man who took a dull butter knife and stabbed me over and over until it successfully broke the skin and muscle and sliced straight to the heart. How am I supposed to put my best foot forward? I never much liked the holiday prior to Mason wrecking my world, but now? The day might as well be another dull butter knife to the heart.

And on top of that? The woman in the campaign will be the drop-dead-gorgeous Genevieve Rhodes?

It's all excruciating. Because regardless of everything that man has done and said to me, I still love him. And that is my toxic trait, friends.

I need to set aside my emotions, which I'm letting get the best of me lately. I have a job to do and a boss who's putting a lot on the line for me. This campaign is a big deal and, if what Hadley says is correct, could put us on the national map, not only as a jewelry company but also as a chic, southern boutique. I wanted to stay on here after I graduated, but now, staying on looks even more promising as I envision years and years of marketing campaigns for a national brand.

Mason Kane, and the dreaded Valentine's Day campaign, will not steal my hopes, dreams, and ambitions from me. I finish dabbing concealer under my eyes and then set my shoulders square.

I can do this.

Chapter Six

♥

Karoline - Present

"I CAN'T DO THIS." I spin around and start darting back towards the boutique. Hadley grabs my forearm and yanks me back. I trip over my beige block-heeled booties and smash into her chest.

After a momentary groan, she says, "You *can* do this, Karoline. Repeat after me: I'm a bold, powerful tiger." Hadley puffs her chest out and tilts her chin in the air, placing her fists on her hips. Passersby on the sidewalk outside of Books and Beans throw curious looks at my carefree boss.

I let out an exasperated laugh. "You may be, especially since you are wearing a crop top with tiger prints, but I'm definitely not. Nope. I'm a timid turtle, much happier to slip into my shell at the first sign of danger." I raise my shoulders to my ears while scrunching my neck downward into my beige turtleneck to prove my turtleness to Hadley.

"Ahaha." Hadley throws her head back and clutches her stomach in mock laughter before straightening her spine, crossing her arms, and narrowing her blue eyes at me. She does this one eyebrow raise thing that always sends a small chill down my spine. "Ma'am. I'm going to need you to express some confidence before I send you into Books and Beans for the meeting. I need to know my employee is going to be okay."

The way her voice softens at the end of her words and how she relaxes her face into a sympathetic expression tells me that she's worried for me. Not going to lie, I'm worried for me, too. I have no idea how I'll react to Mason. The way I reacted to seeing him at Hadley's wedding was to ditch the reception and vomit outside of the car on the side of the road on my drive home. I hadn't even spoken to him then. He looked at me once, but I don't think he recognized me.

I had a similar response on New Year's Eve, but I did get some satisfaction that my tires threw rocks at him, which was not an emotionally secure reaction.

And at the cafe a few days ago, I allowed pent-up anger to consume me and was, admittedly, spiteful towards him. God convicted me about that one while I tried to fitfully fall asleep that night. While I have every right to be angry and displeased with him, I don't have the right to take my frustrations out on him... even if they all stem from his egregious words and actions three years ago.

I can be firm with him, vocalizing my frustrations in a respectful way when necessary, but I can't be intentionally vicious or mean. I have to—are you listening all the way in Dallas, Mom?—be the bigger and better person. This meeting is for my project, which I absolutely have to nail in order to get a good grade in my internship class. My advisor is known for his hardline, meticulous grading, and I don't want to risk my status as valedictorian of the graduating class because of a three-year-old hurt.

That settles it. I won't give him a reason to back out of this marketing campaign, mess up Hadley's business plans, and ruin my perfect GPA. I will play nice and be professional with Mason Kane while we work together on this project, but once it's over, I'll (respectfully but thoroughly) tell him to get the h-e-double-hockey-sticks out of my life.

I blow my bangs from my eyes. "I'm really okay, Boss Lady. I can set my personal issues aside for work and get done what needs to get done. I can't promise I won't go home and scream at the walls after talking to Mason, but I'll be professional when I am in his presence as long as we are working on this campaign." There. That should satisfy her.

"Okay, Karoline. But instead of screaming at the walls, please feel free to come scream with me. Or, as a matter of fact," she pulls her phone from the back pocket of her white-washed jeans, "I'm sure Lucy and Lorelei would love to have you over. Let's plan for that tonight?"

I laugh, already imagining what the twins would say. "Yeah, I could use a girls' night after this meeting."

Hadley beams. "Great! I'll get all the plans made. You just go be your brilliant, beautiful, fierce self and get this campaign off the ground for our store."

Tears prickle at the corner of my eyes. "Our store?"

Hadley draws me in for a hug. "Yes. Our store. Which I need to get back to now. Are you sure you're good?"

I nod, emboldened by the sentiment Hadley shares. *Our store.* I will represent it well. And with that, I push through the glass door of the coffeeshop with the cutest bookstore attached to it and make my way to a small table that seats four. I need to make sure there is plenty of space between me and Mason for this work. Genevieve won't be joining us today as she has a concert, but she will be here in two weeks to start the filming process. Until then, I'll correspond with her agent via email.

Speaking of agents, why am I not meeting with Mason's agent? Shouldn't he be the one handling all of this stuff? I guess Mason knows he's meeting with me and is out to make this coffee shop my personal form of hell for the foreseeable future.

After setting my tablet down, along with other paper materials I need for the meeting, I walk up to the wide, chestnut, wooden counter and look over the specials for the day scribbled in chalk next to the muffins and bagels. The drinks are still New Year's themed as it is only about a week into January, so I order one of my seasonal favorites: Cacao Kisses, a black tea blend with hints of cacao, vanilla, and truffle.

I might as well drink all the tea from here that I want to while I can. I won't be able to step foot in this place once they start decorating for Valentine's Day... I get enough of that lovey-dovey nonsense at work. Blah.

Emma Jane, the barista, whom I also go to college with, quickly gets my tea brewing in one of their cute, light green mugs with floral imprints on the side of it.

"Thanks, Emma Jane," I say as I grab my mug and reluctantly head back to the table in one of the more darkened corners of the café. It's a cloudy day with a storm brewing on the horizon, so the café isn't as lit up as it usually is at ten in the morning. The meeting is for ten-fifteen, but I got here early to make sure I could choose the seats and set the tone. Mason will not pull one over on me today. Nope, I am prepared, and I am a fierce tiger, as Hadley would say.

Chuckling at the thought, I disregard it. While Hadley may be a tiger, I am definitely more of the turtle variety. That wasn't a lie.

The bells above the door jingle, and I jump out of my seat, heart racing.

But it isn't Mason. It is an elderly gentleman who frequents this place as much as I do.

Jeez, Karoline. Not as prepared as you thought you were, huh? Get it together!

My phone buzzes, and I check the screen.

> **Channel:** Good luck today! Show that turd who the real boss is.

I chuckle, sending a heart and thumbs up emoji while my heart rate still comes down from the blasted door opening.

As soon as the beating slows and I go back to sipping my delicious chocolate-tasting tea while looking over the marketing plans Hadley and I had spent the past few days developing, the door opens again.

And once again, my body betrays me, revealing how I *really* feel.

I'm not, in fact, cool as a cucumber, as every romance novel ever written would suggest. At least, that's what Lucy Spence says. It's a rule. The phrase must appear once. I'm not a huge reader, though, so I wouldn't know.

Embarrassingly enough, this whole "door opens, Karoline freaks out" thing happens three more times as ten-fifteen approaches and sweeps by. By ten-twenty, I am anxiously tapping my foot on the floor and hugging the mug of tea close to my lips, mostly to hide part of my face so that if he's looking my direction when he saunters in, maybe I have a fleeting chance of not revealing the anxiety coursing through my veins.

Where is he?

The moment the thought crosses my mind, the bells jingle and the door opens again. This time, a tall, muscular-defined man walks in wearing faded, ripped jeans, a beige Henley long sleeve shirt, and dark brown boots that look to be a masculine Chelsea-style. His hair, a dark chocolate color that sits at the baseline of his neck and, well, flows as he walks towards me, is lucious enough that every woman that sees it wants to run her hands through it.

Every woman but me, that is, because that's the man who ripped my heart out and stomped on it when he left me sitting in a dusty diner in Dallas after effectively ruining me for all men.

Dirtbag.

But look at that full beard he now sports. I definitely noticed it on New Year's Eve, which is why I didn't realize it was him immediately. Imagine that pressed against my cheeks with his lips...

KAROLINE RENEE WRIGHT! He is the devil, girl. And don't you forget it.

He lowers his black sunglasses as he approaches the edge of the table. "Hey, Karoline. Nice scowl you're wearing. Did you mean to accompany it with a sliver of drool?" He motions to the corner of his lip, and I chastise my eyes for following his motion. His voice, as I recognized at our last impromptu run-in three days ago, is deep and rich, a different type of melodic than his singing voice.

His comment and smirk start the process of boiling my blood, but I take a deep breath and remember that I'm the one in charge here. *I'm the boss.* "Mason. It's good to see you," I lie through my teeth. I wish I never had to see him in person again, but Hadley and the Lord seem to have other plans. "Please, have a seat." I gesture to the chair across the table from me, the one that would leave him facing the wall.

I tried to be considerate, knowing he would need to face the wall instead of the other tables. But there was no way I was going to meet with him alone at his house. Nor was I going to let him come to mine. I could have met with him at work, but that still felt too personal. No, we needed to be on neutral ground, hence, the coffee shop. He's obviously comfortable coming here since he was here the other day.

"It's good to see you, too, Karoline." He sets his sunglasses on the table in front of him. We stare at each other from across the table. I take note of his sharpened cheekbones and the full beard, the same dark color as his hair. His shoulders are broader, and his biceps are…

Nope. We aren't looking at how his biceps make that thin shirt look like it's going to pop like a can of Pilsbury biscuits.

Nor are we going to discuss the fact that we are matching and how it low-key thrills me.

I'll burn this sweater when I get home.

Mason's eyes, though, throw me into a time traveling machine and take me back to childhood days when we chased each other around with the garden hose and jumped on soapy trampolines. The warm, deep brown—almost-onyx—color of his irises are reminiscent of summer days spent throwing a softball around or sitting under the shade tree while he wrote music and I painted landscape portraits.

Shaking my head, I refocus on the present. No sense in entertaining a past that's been tainted and tarnished by unrequited love and drunken mistakes. Instead of meeting his eyes, I stare at his forehead. "Hadley Rawls, my boss, says you will be starring alongside Genevieve Rhodes in our marketing campaign for Valentine's Day. She couldn't be here today but will be available in two weeks when we begin filming. I have most of the plans developed, so what I need for you to do is look over them and give your approval." I toss a packet of papers in front of him, causing his sunglasses to slide off the clear-coated table and onto the floor.

Sorry.

Not.

"Hm," he says, bending to pick up his Ray Bans. As he rights himself, my eyes catch his once again. He's still burning memory holes into my brain, memories of water balloon fights, late night jam sessions under the stars, and him cheering me on from the stands, wearing my number, as I played in the Texas state softball game my senior year of high school.

"What?" I ask, forcing my eyes to look anywhere but at him.

"So that's it? You're going to hand me a packet to read over and then leave?" His voice lowers. "Can't we catch up or something?" It sounds like a plea.

The blood that was beginning to boil earlier reaches maximum heat in an instance. "Really, Mason? Catch up? I'm pretty sure the way you drunk-kissed me, said the awful things you said, then left me in that diner, never contacting me again, signified that you no longer wanted anything to do with me."

"Vroom, that was never—"

"Don't call me that!" I shout. Several heads turn our direction, and I bring my voice back down and begin to lean over the table, the edge cutting into my ribs. "Just so we are clear, you don't deserve to get to know how I am or what I've been up to or who my friends are or what degree I'm pursuing. It's bad enough you know where I work and the town I live in. I am working on this project for my job, not to reconnect with you. Got it?"

My chest heaves as I fight to regain control of my emotions, my breaths ragged and deep.

Mason stands then leans on the table, his shades between his fingers while his hands splay on the surface, his face a little too close to mine. Even the daisies in the clear vase serving as the centerpiece on the table shudder at his overwhelming and intense presence. "Look, I'm sorry. I should have led with that. You heard the song. I meant every word. I'm sorry for what I did three years ago, for what I said. I didn't mean any of it. You have to know that, Kar. I'm sorry for dropping in on you unexpectedly like this. Please, forgive me, Karoline. Please…"

His words are three years too late.

I slump back in my chair and cross my arms and legs, turning to the side so that I don't have to look at him. "I don't think I'm capable of forgiving you, Mason. It's not a cut; it's a bullet hole. The wound is too big and too deep. The best I can do, all I've been trying to do, is forget."

Mason swallows, shifting his eyes to the wall behind me and then back to me. "Would it help if I told you that I was stupid for not appropriately returning your feelings? I mean, think about it, I kissed you. Yes, I was drunk. Yes, I blamed it on that. Then you took a shot at my fragile ego and I said a lot of things I regret. But really? I kissed you because I wanted to. I wanted you. After I left, I realized I'd made the most idiotic mistake of my life. Would it help if I told you something that I know is three years too late but is still true as I sit here in front of you? Karoline, I love—"

"No!" I bark, snapping around in my seat and jolting to my feet. "Stop, Mason. You're making fun of me now, aren't you? You didn't humiliate me enough already? Now you have to mock my feelings? Well, news alert, Mr. Conceited, I don't feel that way anymore, okay? I've moved on."

"Yeah, sure you have," he mumbles under his breath while crossing his arms, mirroring my posture. "I don't believe that. I can still read you like an open book. The way your face is flushed, the way you keep avoiding eye contact, and when we make it, you avert your gaze. All the little things you used to do…"

Oh, this infuriating man! "Yeah, I *have* moved on as a matter of fact. You just can't accept that, can you? You just need me falling all over you like a fan girl, but guess what, you—" I stop my sentence, careful not to finish with the curses brimming on my tongue. *Thank you, Lord, for holding my tongue.*

He's not worth it.

I pick up the papers from the table, stare him directly in the eyes, shove the stack into his chest, and paste a smile to my face. "Here are the marketing plans. Read over them and we will meet again on Monday to finalize. Have a nice weekend, and thank you for working with Tease Jewelry and Southern Grace Boutique and Gift Market."

With that, I grab my tablet, my empty mug, and what's left of my dignity and march out of the coffee shop to start heading towards the boutique. I'm pleased with my exit, until I realize I never placed the empty mug onto the dirty dishes tray on the far end of the counter.

Well, rats.

I turn around at the edge of the shop and creep back inside. With my chin held high, I gently drop the mug into the bin, bid a polite farewell to Kelsey, and exit the building once more. I sneak a peek back inside as I pass the windows, and I catch sight of Mason, with his sunglasses back in place, standing by the window with a ridiculous full grin of pretty, perfect teeth, shaking his head and watching me walk by.

That shred of dignity I had left?

It's left in the dirty dishes bin with the mug.

As I walk back to the boutique, which is a couple of blocks down Main Street, my phone vibrates in my pocket.

Do Not Call. Do Not Text. Forget He Exists: I look forward to working with you this Valentine's Day, Vroom. Love, Peppermint.

I wasn't aware my blood could possibly boil anymore, but alas, Mason Kane found a way to turn up the heat and make it happen. How unfortunate that he had kept my number… but I guess I had kept his, too.

Chapter Seven

♥

Mason - Present

WARS ARE NEVER WON in a day.

And getting Karoline Wright to accept my apology (and confession) could take centuries. But I don't have centuries, so I decided to consult with the Prince of Hearts himself as I continue to stare at the opened message I sent Karoline after our meeting earlier today.

"So yeah, that's how the meeting went," I finish telling my roommate about my encounter with Karoline. After she surprised me when I was with him and Braxton at Books and Beans earlier in the week, I was forced to tell the guys everything as we gathered for our Meatball Monday night. All the nitty gritty details better left in the past, the ones that painted me to be the heartless monster that Karoline believes that I am, were spilled over three different types of meatballs and beer.

Well, Braxton and Finley had beer. I had orange juice as I vowed to never drink again after what happened with

Karoline. They didn't know about that vow, though, or I know they would have refrained. I have to admit, it's nice to be around men who know how to respectfully consume alcohol instead of how I did in high school and college.

Finley runs a hand through his shaggy, light blond hair while leaning back on the arm of the couch with one leg crossed over the other. "I don't know how you'll dig your way out of that gargantuan hole, Mason. You seem to only be armed with a kid-size plastic beach shovel if you think confessing on the spot like that is going to win her over."

I stare at him in disbelief from across the room on the reclining chair. The fireplace crackles in the background, filling the log cabin with enough heat to keep me warm in my basketball shorts and t-shirt. Finley, as if he dresses in nothing less than photo-ready attire, wears black dress slacks with a white button up tucked in. He's scrapped the tie, however, and the top two buttons hang open on his shirt.

"What do you mean? Surely you have advice for me?"

He scoffs. "You act as if I actually am a Prince of Hearts. You forget that most of the accusations regarding my dating history are falsified for that press photographer scoundrel Brett Farce to ring money out of my family."

"So you say." I narrow my eyes. Finley simply shrugs then goes about picking up the book on the floor beside the couch: some nonfiction text about European law. "Before you jump into your book, could you at least help me brainstorm a solution? Quite frankly, I don't want to wait a week to see her again."

"Lovestruck fool." Finley laughs, setting the book down in his lap. "I think you need to give her space and time. You've known she's been here all this time, but she had no idea you have been sleazing about town and lurking in dark corners like a full-fledged stalker just to get a glimpse of her. She needs time to come to grips with the fact that you're here and now working alongside her."

I grunt. "I don't like that solution. I'm not a patient man."

Finley rolls his eyes. "You're twenty-four, Mason. And she's twenty-one. There is no rush."

"Do you think I should text her what I wanted to say at the café? That I love her?" I scratch my head, and Finley chokes on the water he just sipped.

"Are you insane?"

I shrug. "It might be the only way she'll hear me out."

"No, not sufficient. When you put your best foot forward for a lady, you show up. You don't hide behind a blasted screen." He mumbles under his breath in Korsan, which sounds like a blend of Swedish and Norwegian.

Throwing my hands up at the clearly insulted prince, I say, "Sorry, sorry. Noted. It was mostly a joke anyway."

He shakes his head. "I leave for Korsa tomorrow, Mason. You're on your own. I won't have time to text you to make sure you're not doing anything rash or stupid. Get it together. I want to see you get your girl back."

"I said I'm sorry," I huff, blowing a strand of hair out of my face. "Again, just joking."

But how will I get Karoline to trust me enough to hear me out? I came here to Mississippi—to Juniper Grove—with the hopes that she wouldn't slip away from me again. I reckoned it'd be hard. I figured she wouldn't trust me, but honestly, I didn't anticipate the utter hatred she seems to have for me. What I did to her was wrong on all possible levels, but I was newly twenty-two. Naïve. Drunk for the last time. It's amazing what three years and living on your own can do to a man.

I saw Karoline for the first time again at Braxton's wedding, and I could see the disdain burning in her eyes as she looked at me from across the sea of people in the backyard of Hadley's house. She left not long after. It was then that I knew it would be no easy feat to reconcile with her.

"Mason?"

Crawling out of my own head, I nod towards Finley, indicating for him to go ahead.

"Invite her out to do something where it's just the two of you, though I'd recommend steering clear of any diners that would give her unwanted flashbacks to three years ago. Don't try to confess your feelings for her but work on reestablishing some sort of friendship. She's not going to trust you easily, so you need to show up for her, and when she doubts you, which will be inevitable, you need to reassure her with your actions, not with your words, that you are a changed man who has his priorities straight."

I stare slack-jawed at the man who casually dropped the world's greatest advice to men everywhere in the middle of this dusty, ambient living room while rain pelts the tin roof. It is the greatest and most obvious advice. "That's uh," I chuckle with embarrassment. I should have thought of that. "That's solid, reasonable counsel."

"Honestly, I thought of what my little sister, Astrid, would tell me in this precarious situation. She's Karoline's age, and quite mature for it. It seems like your Karoline might be as well, despite letting her anger get the better of her."

My stomach tightens as the urge to defend her comes about. "It's my fault she's angry. She has every right to let it out and dish it to me. She's not to blame for that."

Finley smiles. "Very well. I'm aware of that. Just making outsider observations. You are indeed a knuckleheaded boy deserving of a woman's wrath."

"Don't you have some packing to do?"

He picks his book up from his lap and opens it. "No. I finished packing earlier today. I have all night available to read this riveting text on law while simultaneously teasing you."

I strip my socks from my feet and ball them up, flinging them at his face as I stand to grab a cup of water. Finley hurriedly blocks them with his book, and one falls into his glass of water sitting beside the couch.

"While you're up, please get me a clean glass of water."

"No can do, Fins." I open the fridge and pull out the pitcher. "You have all the time in the world, anyway."

He sighs, then I hear his book snap shut. Regardless of my comment, I pour two glasses of water and meet him in the kitchen to hand one off to him.

"Thanks," he mumbles before turning around and going back to his spot on the couch.

I sit back down on the recliner and start thinking about ways to win Karoline's trust back. It won't be easy, but I know her better than I know anyone else, even if it has been three years.

Opening social media, I scroll through Karoline's profile; her username, @karsalwayswright, is permanently etched into my search bar. I browse through old posts, my brain having already memorized many of them from late nights touring when the ache in my chest at missing her was too much to handle.

This one picture always got to me: she's standing on a cliffside of red, clayish dirt with her back to the camera but her head thrown over her shoulder in a carefree, joyful manner. She's wearing black athletic shorts, a red stretchy tank top, and black hiking boots with a floral backpack in tow. Her long legs are tanned, scraped, and a little dirty from her hike. But it's the tattoo peeking out from behind her shirt, just below her neckline that throws me into a tizzy… a peppermint that looks to be a heart etched into the center. I can't be sure, though, because it disappears beneath the red fabric of her tank.

One thing's for sure: Karoline Wright has a peppermint tattoo on her body, and that fact alone leaves my emotions more tangled up than a group of people playing Twister. Despair, joy, guilt, and something akin to hope swims through my veins, and I take a moment to pray to God that by some small miracle, that tattoo signifies that Karoline has some love for me buried deep down underneath all her mounds of wrath.

Tucking my phone away, I grab my guitar and strum, thinking about the blessings the Lord has given me. I thank Him for the chance to reconcile with Karoline, even if it isn't quite the way I was expecting to. I'll have to work for her, and that's okay.

Dancing stars, full moon of possibilities. You're here in my arms again, this night can never end…

Setting my guitar aside, I jot down the lyrics in my notebook app on my phone.

Chapter Eight

♥

Karoline - Three Years Ago

J UST CALL ME ROTISSERIE Chicken.

The July Texas heat has roasted me to a golden brown with my internal body heat blazing at a good thousand degrees.

That's a lie, of course, but it sure feels that way as I stand underneath the bright sun. Even the brownish-blue lake water that's up to my chest is too warm for comfort, and the mud at the bottom of the lake squishes warmly between my toes. But Mason wanted to swim, and he's the one who took his last shot with that girl from college and was turned down at the Morgan Wallen concert a couple of days ago (yay for me!), so I'm doing whatever he wants today.

"Heads up, Vroom!"

I snap my head to the left in time to stare wide-eyed at Mason swinging through the air. He's holding on to a thick, dirty rope with his ankles wrapped around a knot towards the bottom of the redneck contraption.

Oh, but it's just a rope swing? How's that redneck? I'm glad you asked…

This rope swing is dangling not only on a cliff, but from the top of a crane buried into the cliff.

Mason doesn't let go as he reaches maximum distance. He volleys back towards the crane and pushes off the metal arms with his feet before wrapping them around the knot again. With the added momentum, his placement is…

SPLASH!

Mason lands not even a foot away from me, barely making it far enough to reach the drop off. Water floods me like the storm surge in a hurricane, stinging my eyes, invading my mouth, and shooting up my nose. While I'm coughing and spitting the nasty liquid from my system, hands grab my ankles, and I'm dragged under the surface and off the drop off.

With all the force I can muster, I kick at Mason (because I know there are no mermaids dragging me down in this lake) until he lets me go and I swim upwards, my lungs burning for air. I'm skilled at many things, but holding my breath for any small length of time is not one of them. In fact, I always pray that when I die, it won't be from suffocation.

Someone *is* about to die from strangulation, though…

"Mason Jonathan Kane!" Water droplets fly from my mouth as I shout his name, peddling my way back to ground. He catches me from behind, his arms wrapping around my waist as he yanks me backwards and into his chest.

My body, all smashed up against a wet, shirtless Mason, decides its new response to fight or flight is to simply freeze. With my back feeling every ounce of bare chest he has to offer and my hormones still wanting more, I tilt my head back, fitting it perfectly against the nape of his neck.

Then I'm submerged under the water again.

What is with this guy? Is he so angry with that college girl that he's resorted to drowning me?! No, sir. I don't think so.

Fight mode resumes and I kick and punch my way out of his grip, bobbing back to the surface and swimming backwards towards land. Mason swims after me, laughing like a maniac. The wicked gleam in his dark chocolate eyes and the way his thick hair falls in wet strands providing a pretty frame for his pretty face is raining confusion down onto my nervous system. The woman in me wants to succumb to the handsome man prowling towards me while my logical half screams to get to safety.

I choose safety, crawling onto what we call "the Beach"—a small, rocky-sandy area with a few folding chairs and a fire pit where water meets land. I get out of the water and plop down into the oversized red outdoor chair.

"You'd think I was actually out to kill you by the way you were reacting, Vroom." Mason slushes out of the lake—droplets of water sparkling like diamonds rolling down his chest—and sits in the blue chair next to me, his maniacal laugh still fully intact. When I don't answer, he shifts from laughter into a low, seductive drawl. "Come on, *little ma'am*. Don'tcha trust me?"

Does he mean for that to be seductive? Or is my brain still on high alert from our bodies pressed together? It's not the first time he's called me "little ma'am," but he rarely uses it, and when he does, it rewires my brain a little more to be attuned to only him.

"I don't trust you as far as I can throw you," I jest, purposefully turning my head away from the handsome man. He has no right to look that good fresh out of nasty lake water.

"Well, have I ever lied to you? Stolen from you? Harmed you in any way?"

Yes, you've stolen my heart, which is quite harmful. "No. But that doesn't mean I have to trust you when it comes to your version of 'joking around.'" I risk a glance, and he's mocking offense by slapping a hand over his heart. I stand up, climb the short hill to our four wheeler, and grab my baggy t-shirt, his shirt, and my water bottle.

"You leaving me now?" he yells.

"Grabbing clothes," I holler back.

When I return, he's still sitting in the chair, looking smug as he leans to one side and wears a smirk. I toss him his shirt, tugging mine on over my olive green sports bra and matching workout shorts—my chosen swim attire.

As I'm sitting back down, he says, "What? Is all this too much for you?" He gestures down his body.

Yes.

"Ha, as if." *As if it isn't…*

"Aw, come on, Vroom. You know I'm sexy."

"I know you're conceited."

He leans over, his forearms resting on his knees. "Well, I, for one, am glad you put the shirt on. I'll honestly say you're attractive. Especially in olive green…"

The water I sipped on as he began talking comes spewing out in a coughing fit. It takes a moment for me to catch my breath from choking on the liquid. "I'm sorry. *What* did you just say to me?"

He leans back with a shrug, a smirk still playing on his lips. I'm glad he can't tell a blush from a sunburn on my face right now.

"You're attractive. It's a simple fact. You should know this."

While my brain celebrates Mason's confession, I try to calm myself down. He said I was attractive, which I know is true, but hearing it come from him… It's the best compliment regarding my looks I've ever received. But he never said he liked me in a romantic way, only that my good looks were factual.

Nope. Nothing romantic about a statement like that.

"Thank you," I whisper.

"No compliment in return? I'm hurt."

I roll my eyes. "Ah, so that's what this is. You got your pride hurt by Cassidy and now you're fishing for validation to nurse your wounds."

The way his shoulders tense and the playful expression falls from his face tells me that I might not be far off the mark with my retort.

"Just joking." I rush the words trying to play the comment off.

He snickers through a tight smile, standing to his full six-foot-one height. "Well, Vroom. I think you just unintentionally took my ego down a notch and diagnosed the problem."

An uncomfortable feeling settles over me at his admission. Did he not mean that he thinks I'm pretty, then? I shake the selfish thought process away. "That was quick self-reflection."

He relaxes and lets out a genuine chuckle. "I've got some emotional intelligence inside this male brain of mine. And I can tell by your scrunched nose and the dimple between your brows that you don't think I meant what I said earlier. So let me be clear, *little ma'am.*" Twice in one day? Heaven help me…

Mason takes a few steps in my direction, squats down in front of me, and reaches out his hand to pluck a wet strand of hair from my cheek. His eyes are soft but intense. His touch is… Don't even get me started on the way his calloused fingertips feel scratching against my cheek. "Though I was teasing you, you have to know that you *are* attractive, Karoline. Never doubt that."

I didn't realize I had insecurity issues until the moment they disappeared at Mason's firm, straightforward words. With him still squatting in front of me, I place my hand on his rounded, sculpted shoulder. The heat that burns through the shirt at the touch could warm an Alaskan village in January.

"Thanks, Peppermint. And for the record," I swallow the fear rising in my throat as I make a love confession disguised as a friendly confidence boost, "you are amazing. Cassidy is insane for not returning your feelings. Any woman out there would be hashtag blessed to call you theirs. You've got charm, charisma, good looks, intelligence—apparently the emotional kind, too—and you can sing. You're a catch, Mason Kane. Don't let someone else take that confidence from you."

His lips pull into a beautiful, big smile as he stands. He wraps his arms underneath my armpits and lifts, jerking me to my feet. When he tugs me into a bear-hug, I can't breathe, and it's not because he's holding me too tight.

It's because I don't think I can handle not telling this man how I truly feel much longer. I'm tired of stifling the three words I want to scream.

I want to make him mine…

He whispers against my ear, "Green *is* my favorite color."

Chapter Nine

♥

Karoline - Present

A TONGUE PIERCING COULD be cool.

"Yeah, I'd do it. That sounds less painful than trying to write a book. No offense, Luce."

The freckled, petite red-head shrugs. "You're not wrong. Okay, Lor. Would you rather eat McDonald's once a day for a week or never purchase another plant ever again?"

We all shift our eyes to Lorelei, who is deep in thought—too much so if you ask me. To any other person, the answer would be obvious. But for Lorelei Spence, choosing is proving to be as difficult as I assume her twin meant it to be.

Finally, she says, "I have over thirty plants between here and my office. As long as I continue to take good care of them, I feel I could be satisfied never buying another one. But eating McDonald's for a week sounds like a death wish. So, I'm going to go with never buying another plant."

"I would choose Micky D's no matter the other option. Their fries are delicious! Especially dipped in barbeque sauce." Hadley grins while Lorelei scrunches her face in disgust. "Okay, your turn, Luce. Would you rather be single forever or never publish your books?"

"Does it sound bad if I say I'd rather never publish? I love my stories, don't get me wrong, but I would much rather live a lifelong romance than write fictional ones." She sighs. "But until that moment comes, I'll continue to write and eventually publish."

"That doesn't sound bad." I place my hand on Lucy's shoulder. "I think most of us women would rather live a romance than read or write about it."

"Ten out of ten recommend," Hadley pipes in with a giggle. Lucy shoves against her. Across from me, Lorelei twiddles her fingers. She's the only one to have never had a boyfriend before. I don't think it's on purpose, but I don't know for sure as I've never outright asked her.

The game of Would You Rather continues until the oven dings, indicating our enchiladas are ready. The smell is intoxicating, effectively lighting a fire under my bum to get our mango-flavored mocktail mixed. Hadley doesn't drink due to her past battle with it, so if we are all hanging out with her, we steer clear of any alcoholic beverages.

Once we have all made our plates and have sat down at the circular, white-distressed wooden table, we dig in. Hadley immediately drips enchilada sauce down her white sweater, causing us to all spill sauce in a fit of giggles. She's notorious for spilling her food all over herself when she eats, no matter how careful she is.

"One day," she growls. "One day I will eat a meal without wearing it, too."

"Never gonna happen, Hads." Lucy shoves a spoonful of rice into her mouth.

We continue eating, occasional light conversation taking place between enchilada bites and sips of our mocktails. When we all have empty plates, we each take turns washing our dishes—no sense in leaving the twins with a load to wash considering there isn't a dishwasher in the apartment.

"Okay. Who's down for another game?" Lucy asks.

Hadley yawns. "As much fun as this has been, I think it's time for me to get back home to my hubby."

Lucy and I stick our tongues out playfully at Hadley and her happily married self, but Lorelei steps in and gives her a hug goodbye and says, "I think I'm going to turn in, too. Feel free to stay over, Karoline."

We all exchange hugs and goodbyes, but before Hadley makes it all the way out the door, she says, "Oh! I almost forgot. Lucy, I'm setting you up with my friend, Finley. You met him at the wedding, remember? He's gone back to his home country for a month, but when he comes back, he's already agreed to a blind date with you."

Lucy has to pick her jaw up off the floor. "You're the best, Hads!" She jumps to Hadley for one more hug, then Hadley's out the door.

Lucy and I help Lorelei finish cleaning up the kitchen while Lucy goes on and on about the possibility of marrying a prince. I had no idea he was a prince, but apparently Lucy had social-stalked him after the wedding and found out the secret. The twins still hadn't told Hadley that they knew who he truly was, so I encouraged them to do that soon. Secrets don't make friends, after all.

"Goodnight, ladies. Love y'all," Lorelei says, drying her hands on the kitchen towel. As Lorelei disappears into her room, Lucy and I sprawl out on the small, cocoa-colored loveseat couch, instantly joined by their two Abyssinian cats, Frannie and Frizzle, who had been hiding out in Lorelei's room.

Frizzle hisses at me when I attempt to pet her, but she curls up sweetly in Lucy's lap.

"Don't mind her. She's a brat sometimes." Lucy runs her fingers through Frizzle's coat. Frannie, bless her, allows me to pick her up, set her on my lap, and snuggle her. "Yeah, she's the nicer of the two."

We are sitting there, loving on the cats, when Lucy clears her throat. "So, Mason Kane, huh?"

I almost made it the entire night without the mention of his name. I should have known Lucy was waiting to get us alone.

"I saw you crying on New Year's Eve," I redirect. "I meant to text you but got caught up taking care of my cousin. Everything okay?"

Lucy snickers. "Nice try, girly pop. But we are talking about you. Besides, the story isn't a good one. Just the typical girl-meets-cute guy and said cute guy turns out to be a walking red flag. Girl's previously fantasized dreams are shattered, so she sobs inconsolably over her seriously sucky single life."

"I feel like we need to talk about that."

"I feel like we don't. He was a nobody, but your Mason and your past with him is something worth discussing."

Lucy is someone I can trust without a doubt. I also think she may be the most understanding of my situation as the woman is a hopeless romantic. At the very least, she'll rage with me.

Taking a deep breath, I begin.

"Mason and I grew up together. We were neighbors. He lived with his dad and step-mom—his mom passed when he was in eighth grade—in the house next to mine in a small suburban neighborhood in Dallas, and I lived with my parents. Since neither of us had siblings, we naturally bonded together. He went to a local high school while I was homeschooled, so I needed him more than he needed me, I think. We quickly became best friends, nearly inseparable on the weekends and during the summer months. When he went off to college, we'd text constantly and spend most of the breaks together.

"The summer after I graduated high school, he was preparing to enter his junior year of college. But, instead of continuing college, one of his songs that he uploaded to social media went viral. Overnight, he had multiple record companies reaching out to him, and his other songs started climbing the viral ranks."

"'Boyfriend Without Benefits'?" Lucy presumes. I nod. Lucy tilts her head for me to continue.

"I was there when he wrote that song, you know? I was behind the camera when he created the video." For some unknown reason, I find myself fighting the urge to cry.

Lucy's expression softens. I snuggle Frannie closer, who is being a very good cat right now by tolerating my unabating squeezes.

"Anyway, I obviously fell in love with him at some point during our childhood. He went from being a hero figure in my eyes to someone I wanted to kiss. After I solidified my feelings and knew they weren't a fluke, I decided to confess. I didn't have to wait long to see him. He invited me out late one night to a twenty-four hour diner we frequented. This was the night before his song went viral. We ordered milkshakes—him chocolate and me strawberry—and a basket of fries to share. I mustered up all the confidence I could create and told him how I felt about him… that I loved him."

After a prolonged pause, Lucy exclaims, "And?!"

"We were in a corner booth in the back, he was sitting across from me though it was a connected bench seat. He slid up next to me and kissed me."

Lucy howls in victory, and both of the cats arch out of our hands and sprint away. I shift my position, tucking the opposite leg than before under my butt. Telling this story again for the first time in two years isn't as difficult as I imagined it would be, but I'm just now getting to the most painful part. My stomach clenches, threatening to churn up the enchiladas from earlier.

"Don't celebrate prematurely," I warn. Her smile immediately falls.

"What happened?"

"When he slid in beside me, I smelled it on him. Alcohol. And when his lips forcefully overtook mine, I wanted to vomit at the taste of beer mingled with chocolate in his saliva."

Lucy folds her legs underneath her. "Oof. That's rough."

"Tell me about it. I pushed him away and asked him what he thought he was doing. As much as I wanted him, I sure as heck wasn't going to have him like that. I know my worth, and it wasn't as low as settling for someone who wanted me only because I wanted him."

Lucy cheers. "That's my girl! But what did he say back to you?"

I freeze, willing the words to stay burned away in the metaphorical memory hole I tossed them into. "I don't want to talk about that, if that's okay."

"Of course," Lucy hurriedly says. "So, was that your first kiss?"

"Yep." I pop my "P," a habit I've stolen from Hadley. "I don't know how I didn't realize he was inebriated beforehand; I chalked it up to the fact that I was nervous about confessing and ruminating over what I would say to him. But there he was, stealing my very first kiss while alcohol laced his brain."

The memory is potent. I can still smell the soured state of his breath, feel the shiver running down my spine even while sweat trickled down my skin. The way his hands tangled with and yanked my hair as he gripped my face to drag his lips to mine still caused a dull ache in my skull. The dust on the window sill of the back corner booth we occupied, the condensation on the window created by the air conditioned interior to combat the wicked July heat, the low chatter of people around us enjoying life while my world upended... It all felt like yesterday.

"Wow. Men... I swear. They think they can use us for whatever need they want to fill when we express the slightest interest." Lucy scowls, and I nod in agreement.

"So that's what happened. And seeing him earlier today for our first of several meetings together was difficult, to say the least. I'm glad Hadley decided to ask you guys to hang out tonight. I needed it more than you know."

Lucy stands and pulls me to my feet, then she embraces me in a tight, warm hug that has a calming effect on my heightened nerves. As my body relaxes, the tears I had been battling fall freely and continuously, soaking the shoulder of Lucy's favorite baby pink sweater that reads: *Whatever you do or say may end up in a novel.*

"Sorry." I sniffle as I break the hug. I rub my eyes, thankful I took my work makeup off before coming up here tonight. "I guess I didn't realize how much I needed to talk about it. Hadley was right, talking about it is healing in its own way."

"I know there's not much I can do to help, but I'm always a listening ear when you need to let something out. You're safe with me." Lucy hugs me again, and I chuckle when she kisses my ear. She's such a wonderful weirdo sometimes.

"Thanks, Luce. Now, how about we find those scaredy cats of yours, snuggle up with popcorn, and watch a movie?"

"Sounds like a plan. Oh, do you want to hear about the latest novel I'm working on? I'm dabbling in urban fantasy. It has to do with a female pirate and a merman, though I think I want to make the merman a prince," she winks, "because I might have my very own prince soon enough."

As Lucy excitedly tells me about her new story idea, with mingling commentary of Prince Finley Andersson, I become one with the couch, comforted by the fact that I have a community of amazing women surrounding me. Something I never had during my teen years thanks to homeschooling and attending a church where I was one of three youths at any given moment. This sisterhood is beautiful, and I never want to lose it. I don't need Mason or his friendship or his apologies. In fact…

Mason Kane can kiss my butt.

Chapter Ten

❤

Mason - Present

M Y FINGER HOVERS OVER the "send" button.

I crafted a well-thought-out text to send to Karoline, inviting her to go hiking with me out at the Bluffs
this coming weekend. It's been three days since I've seen her
when we met at the coffee shop again to finalize the plans.
I didn't push her, as Finley suggested not to do, and she was
nothing but professional with me, so I gave her the same
energy despite wanting to bring everything up again....
*Despite wanting to flirt with her and use our physical chemistry
to manipulate her feelings.* No, I wouldn't do that. I've grown
from the boy I was three years ago. From here on out, I have
to keep my flirtation in check until she's ready to receive
it. Though, I'll admit, it's going to be more difficult than
setting up the concert stage or hiding from the press.

After the meeting, I ended up driving to Nashville for a
last-minute invite to a charity concert due to another artist
dropping out. They had asked me to participate a while

back, but I said no on the account of taking a break since my tour had concluded. After realizing just how mad Karoline was at me, I decided to accept the invitation to keep myself busy for a couple of days.

But now I am back in Juniper Grove, sitting alone in the cabin, spending over an hour typing and deleting words to send to the woman I love who ardently despises me.

I read over the text again:

Karoline, I don't like the way we left things the other day, and I would truly appreciate the chance to explain. I have no excuse for what happened three years ago, and I promise I will not try to justify my actions. All I'm asking for is the opportunity to apologize sincerely and in person. Would you be willing to go on a hike in the Bluffs with me on Saturday? The weather says it'll be a warmer day with lots of sunshine. I'll pack the snacks. Boston style peanuts. You still like those, right? Think it over. Let me know something by tomorrow evening, please? - Mason

I hadn't meant to type a letter, but this version of my "reaching out text" is bounds and leaps better than the initial *Hey, Vroom. Wanna go on a hike Saturday? We should really talk. You know you miss this handsome face.*

Yeah, I'm ashamed to have written that early, short draft. There's no way under the sun Karoline would have agreed, much less graced my phone with a response. I have to be more for her. Better to her.

That is something I've learned over the past three years. I had always known Karoline was too good for me, but what I failed to realize was that I could be enough for her if I just stopped acting like a conceited tool. There is a time and place for jokes, even conceited ones, and right now is not that time. Right now, I have to focus on gaining a morsel of trust back, then I'll pray my heart out that God will treat that morsel like the loaves of bread and multiply it abundantly.

With a short prayer, I hit send, then I set my phone screen-down on the kitchen counter. Checking the time, my stomach grumbles. I'm two hours late for lunch. My personal trainer would kill me if he found out, so I heat up chicken from yesterday inside the airfryer and season fresh broccoli to pop in the oven to roast.

After shoving my meal down my throat, I slap on extra deodorant and slip into my running shoes. Hesitantly, I grab my phone and flip it over.

No text.

Reminding myself that it's okay—she's probably at work—I unplug my dark green earbuds from the charger and search for my hype playlist, which is basically a collection of 2010s rap songs. When "Black and Yellow" by Wiz Khalifa (the clean version) floods my speakers, a surge of adrenaline races through my system and I take one last swig of water before running out of the house and down the paved street. Braxton doesn't have many neighbors around, but there is a nice elderly man that lives within yelling distance. I usually run earlier in the mornings while he sits out on his porch sipping a drink. We exchange pleasantries as I pass, and he's even invited me over a few times. I've yet to take him up on the offer, but I know I'll need to soon. Especially if I'm staying in this area. I need to be able to trust those who live around me.

I continue to wind down the road, where the farther I get, the less cabins there are. About a mile and a half into my run, I'm at the construction site where my new home is being built. The foundation and framing are finished, so now they're working on the third stage—plumbing, windows, roofing, the works. Making a mental note to come check in with everyone and bring drinks this evening, I continue my jog.

I go another half-mile past my new home then turn around to trek the two miles back. Winded and numb, and apparently lapsing in self control, my thoughts drift to Karoline. The urge to check my phone, which still had notifications silenced, is enticing. One glance could put my burning question at rest.

Right after I pass my house again, I cave. Slowing down to a brisk walk, I slip my phone from my pocket.

Notifications flood my phone from various individuals and companies. I sift through them, looking for the coveted new text message notification. There are several, but none of them belong to Karoline.

I open the thread and re-read the message. It still says delivered, and I don't know if that means she hasn't read it or if she has her read receipt turned off like I do. I click the screen dark then tuck my phone away, forcing my numb legs to pick up the pace.

As my heart pounds, "Trap Queen" by Fetty Wap (also the clean version) blasts through my headphones, and my feet carry me forward. I try and fail to not think about that evening when I did the one thing I swore I'd never do.

Chapter Eleven

♥

Mason - Three Years Ago

"COME ON, MAN. IT'S your birthday! Get over her already." My buddy from college, Nick, pats my back as he takes another swig of beer. HARDY's music pulses through the barn, drowning out many conversations happening around me. The hoots and hollers of beer pong victories echo supreme, however.

Cassidy made it clear that I'll never end up with her. After the Morgan Wallen concert at the beginning of the month, I took my last shot, telling her how I felt, and when she didn't say anything, I took it to mean she was speechless and went in to kiss her. When she dodged my kiss saying I was like a brother to her, I knew it was all over for me.

Ouch. It still stings.

But that's why I've got this beer in my hand. I take a swig, trying to forget the dull ache of my pride being gutted.

I was set on making that beautiful woman mine, but fate has other plans, I guess.

So here I am, in a dusty, stale-smelling, sticky-hot barn in late July trying to catch a numbing buzz while old high school and college friends who came to visit for my twenty-second birthday drink beer, play drinking games, and dance—well, grind—on one another. I didn't ask for the party, but they gathered for one anyway. To them, my birthday is just another occasion to get drunk. But hey, I can't complain. It's what I need right now.

I'm sure Karoline hears the noise across the fence. I'm surprised she hasn't texted me about it yet, but we did hang out earlier this morning at the lake, and I told her some old friends and college friends would be popping in. She didn't seem like herself, now that I think about it. Her usual bubbly, sarcastic persona was gone, in her place, a woman with a timid and quiet spirit.

The Bible says something about how a woman like that is a woman of value, but honestly, I like Karoline with a little feisty energy. It doesn't make her loud or obnoxious or overbearing, no. It makes her radiate, fun to be around, and my favorite person to tease. I don't know if society interprets that passage of scripture correctly, but what do I know? I was born and raised a Christian, but I don't go to church every Sunday, and I don't pray or read my Bible daily. But I can tell you one thing—I like Karoline Wright just the way she is.

And dang it. I wish she was at this party…

Suddenly, there's a shot of amber liquid in my face. "What the…?" Nick stands in front of me wearing athletic shorts and a dirt-stained t-shirt. His curly hair is unruly, sticking up in various ways from running his hands through the damp strands. "Trust me, Mason. You need to lighten up. You look like a stump on a log sitting on that hay bale."

"I don't want to mix," I tell him, but I take the shot from his hands anyway. "This is the only one I'll do."

I throw it back, letting the burn wash down my throat. I'm not much of a whiskey drinker, but it is my birthday, so what the heck…

"Yeah, brother!" Nick shouts. "Now, let's go chat up those pretty blonde friends of Dana." I follow his pointed finger to see two tanned girls dressed in Daisy Duke shorts and crop tops, tossing their hair and sipping on beers as they sway to the music in the barn.

"Maybe one of them will want to date me." I laugh without mirth, then follow Nick's lead, all the while battling a sinking feeling settling in my stomach, the sting of rejection, Karoline's name floating through my thoughts, and the memory of her smile imprinted on my brain.

Two hours later, most of my friends have passed out in various places inside the house. Dad is in Fort Worth on Guard duty and my step-mom went to visit her family in Colorado, so I have the place to myself tonight and the rest of the weekend. He left a cake for me in the fridge, which was sweet of him. Kinda makes me feel guilty about this party since I know he doesn't approve of my drinking habits.

It's not an addiction, just a young man trying to live his life while he can. It won't hurt me, and I can stop anytime I want to.

Right now, the numbness I feel is a celebration of life… nothing else. Even if I was rejected by Cassidy, those other two girls didn't seem to have a problem with me tonight. See? I've still got it. It's Cassidy's loss.

Thinking about Cassidy, for some reason, makes me think about Karoline again and how she told me back at the beach a couple weeks ago that any girl would be "hashtag blessed" to have me. Chuckling at the thought, I grab a plastic cup from the cabinet and stick it under the spout on the fridge. Once the water teeters on the edge of the rim, I carefully move the cup and bring it to my lips for a sip. The cool liquid is refreshing, and I end up guzzling the whole thing down. While refilling my cup again, my phone buzzes in my back pocket.

Vroom:

I set my water down on the kitchen table and turn all my focus on typing, making sure I'm saying what I mean to say instead of texting gibberish since I feel like I'm spinning and spiraling while standing in the darkened kitchen.

Me: Yep. Most of my friends are asleep. The ones who aren't will be soon enough.

I sip my water slower this time, sitting down at the table.

> **Vroom:** That's good. I'm glad you could see your friends. Happy Birthday again, Peppermint.

I don't know if it's the alcohol talking or not, but I ask Karoline if she wants to meet for fries and shakes at Dallas Junction Diner. It's a local diner within walking distance, so it's safe for me to go.

> **Vroom:** Sure. Why not stuff our faces at midnight?

Chugging the rest of my water, I zigzag around bodies laying down on the living room floor, most definitely stepping on hands and legs, until I reach my bedroom where Nick has sprawled out on the bed. I click on the standing lamp and make quick work of changing my clothes. After that, I dart across the hall to the bathroom and brush my teeth, comb my hair, and spritz cologne on my neck and shirt. Before I exit the bathroom, I double check my appearance amidst the occasional spinning of my vision. Nothing inside out, everything matches, and I look put together.

Good.

It's not that Karoline doesn't know I like to have a good time; she chides me over it every opportunity she gets saying that I don't need to do those things just because I'm legally allowed to do so. But something inside me doesn't want her to know the extent to which I have a good time. She's never seen me drunk, and I don't want it to start now. I'm sober enough to hide it well. I've had a lot of practice in college.

The sticky, humid nighttime air clings to my skin as I walk down the sidewalk through the subdivision. The streetlights provide the path through the exit gate, then I cross the street into the parking lot of Dallas Junction Diner. A yellow classic diner sign sits above the small, square building. A few cars are in the lot, and when I look through the glass window front, I see a handful of people spread throughout the diner. I spot Karoline in the back corner booth, and my world tilts as nausea pulls in my stomach.

Oh, that's not good.

Swallowing the feeling down, I open the swing door and enter, the immediate smell of fried food oddly enough settling my stomach. I wave to Gertrude, a woman in her late fifties who likes to work the night shift here, and then slide into the mustard yellow booth opposite Karoline.

I'm careful to keep my distance just in case the smell of alcohol is too strong regardless of my change of clothes.

Karoline flashes a grin at me, and then it disappears as she tucks her chin to her chest. Her wrists rest on the table and she picks at her fingernails, the baby blue paint chipping at the top of her middle finger. Her caramel hair is flowing in big waves over her shoulders, and I appreciate the way it cups her sweet face. She rarely wears it down, and when she does, she starts to look a lot older than eighteen. Especially with the way her cheeks have lost some of their youthfulness over the summer, a slow, subtle change that I unintentionally tracked.

She's beautiful, no doubt. And the alcohol still coursing through my blood is tempting me to do something about my attraction to her.

"You look good for midnight," I blurt, watching as she snaps her head back up and seemingly stares into my soul with her big, deep blue eyes.

"Uh, thanks?"

I run a hand through my hair then take a sip of water Gertrude brought over a moment ago. "No, I mean… It's midnight, but you are wearing a pretty blue sundress and have make up on."

Cassidy wore sundresses all the time…

"Oh, uh, yeah. Well, I was wearing this out to town earlier in the day after you left and I just haven't changed." She sips a strawberry milkshake. "I told Gertrude you were coming. She should have your chocolate shake out soon."

Right on cue, the spritzy older lady sets a tall, rounded glass filled with my favorite flavor milkshake and topped with whipped cream on the table in front of me. I thank her then pop the bright green straw she handed me into the drink. The first cold sip tastes like heaven sliding down my throat, but I know better than to chug it right now. I don't want it coming back up later.

Gertrude then sets a basket of hot fries in front of us, and Karoline and I both reach for the exact same fry, our fingers brushing against each other. The warmth of her skin against mine is something I momentarily wish I could spend forever experiencing. She pulls her hand away first, so I grab a fry and toss it into my mouth, trying not to salivate at the salty goodness.

"Mm. These are the best fries in the world, hands down."

"Agreed," she says, grabbing a handful for herself and setting them on a napkin in front of her. "So, how was your birthday party?"

"Eh, it was all right. Kinda wished you were there." I want to kick myself for letting words out of my mouth before I verify them. Meeting Karoline in this state wasn't my best idea, especially because of my growing attraction to her. I'm good at hiding the buzz, but she knows me. She's going to catch on.

"You could have invited me," she whispers, then sips her shake. As her lips wrap around the blue straw, I envision her puckering up for a kiss and leaning into me…

I cough, shaking the thought away. "Not your scene. You wouldn't have liked it."

"Fair enough."

Silence ensues between us as we sip our drinks and munch on fries. Eventually, Karoline asks, "So, why the impromptu diner dash at midnight?"

I shrug. "We do this a lot. Plus it's my birthday."

"*Was* your birthday," she teases, motioning to the gold chain watch on her left wrist. "It's officially over now."

"And here I was hoping for another gift from you." I wink then catch myself again. *Dang it, Mason. Quit flirting with Karoline. Just because Cassidy rejected you doesn't give you the right to hit on your best friend who you're pretty sure has feelings for you, and… You might reciprocate them. At least to a physical degree.*

"I do have something I want to say," Karoline says, her words jumbled together as she rushes to get them out. "Mason, I—I love you. And I know that may be shocking to hear, but I can't hold it in any longer. I have loved you for a very long time, and this summer, you've been more flirty and have teased me more than you ever have before. I could be totally off the mark here—I don't think that I am—but I think you like me too. Maybe you don't love me, but that's something that can be built. There's something between us. That's for sure. And I really hope I'm not wrong…"

Karoline's anxious gaze burns my body more than the liquor did. She likes me. She loves me. I knew this already; Karoline was never good at hiding her emotions. But she finally admitted it to me…

See, Cassidy? Someone thinks I'm worth loving as more than a friend…

I swore I'd never date Karoline because the woman is way too good for me, she's my best friend, and she's basically like family.

But she isn't family…

And she looks hot in that sundress, confessing her feelings for me…

Maybe I could let the liquor talk just this once…

Without another thought, I stand, slide over in the booth until I'm shoulder to shoulder with Karoline. When she looks up at me with wide eyes and parted lips, the haze of the night takes over and I wrap my hands into her hair, dragging her lips to meet mine.

Chapter Twelve

Karoline - Present

A TTENTION! KAROLINE WRIGHT HAS lost her mind. Reward guaranteed if found.

> **Me:** Okay

I stare at the four-letter word I sent moments ago to Mason's long-winded text inviting me to go hiking. It's Friday, nine o' clock at night, and a small part of me wonders if I was too late in sending the response. I shouldn't care, and I remind myself of that, but it still doesn't stop me from hoping I wasn't too late.

My phone buzzes, and I see a text notification from him and his new name in my phone since, unfortunately, I can't forget he exists at the moment. With embarrassment flooding my cheeks at how quickly I swiped to open the text, I read it.

> **A Cruel Twist of Fate:** Wow, okay! Awesome. I'm glad we get to do this. I'll pick you up from the boutique at seven in the morn-

> ing? I know you don't want me to have your
> address, so will that be okay?

My heart pitter-patters in my chest, and I'm once again flooded with embarrassment. How can I continue to embarrass myself *to* myself? It makes zero sense.

> **Me:** Yeah. Fine.

Regardless of my emotions that I have presumably forgotten how to control when it comes to Mason Kane, I must maintain a barrier built out of anger, frustration, and hurt. Which is easy to do considering I very much feel those emotions. My heart and hormones have minds of their own, but my brain knows all too well what kind of man Mason is. And it will not allow me to go back there.

I thought long and hard over his text, and I spent time in prayer, trying desperately to hear the answer I wanted, which was, "Tell Mason Kane just where he can go!" Of course, God did not answer me in that way, but instead, I felt the Holy Spirit guiding me to certain verses, Ephesians 4:32-33:

"Let all bitterness and wrath and anger and clamor and slander be put away from you, along with all malice. Be kind to one another, tenderhearted, forgiving one another, as God in Christ forgave you."

If I'm being honest, I fought the command like the one time I had to face down a Karen who wanted a refund for jewelry clearly marked with a red sign that read "no returns."

But God, he kissed me without my permission!

But God, he said all of those horrible things to me!

But God, he… The list goes on and on.

Through it all, I remembered that Jesus was hung on a cross by those who despised him, mocked him, and rejected him. Yet, He still prayed for them, asking God the Father to forgive them all.

With assurance that can only come from the Father, I decided I would do the right, Christian thing and hear him out and maybe even accept his apology, but I don't have to forget about what he did and the things he said. Nope. Never. The Bible says God can forget about our sins and transgressions, but it doesn't say I have to forget about the sins committed against me.

My phone rings, pulling me from my thoughts.

I smile. "Hey, Mama."

"Karoline, listen to this…" Mama goes on about a new dish she's trying to cook. I can hear the clanging of pans and slamming of cabinets in the background. I interject with commentary until she's done, and then she settles down and recoups. That's Mama… Always distracted with something. "Oh, what I wanted to call you about is your internship. How's it going? What did Hadley assign you to do?"

My stomach churns. "It's going," I reply. But she pesters me for more information. After I tell her exactly what I'm doing for my internship, she lets out a long breath.

"Well, honey. I think this may be a good thing."

"Excuse me?"

A pause, and then, "I know he hurt you. But we both know that's not who Mason is at his core. And we both know a lot can change in the span of three years. He's a Christian now… a true one, not in name only. You know I love that boy like he's my own son. Just the other day, he sent me…"

As Mama drones on about the things Mason has done for her, how he no longer drinks, how he gave his life to Christ, and so on, I'm stuck wondering why everyone in the world can seem to accept that Mason is a different person but me?

I'm still right where he left me…

"How's Dad?" I redirect the conversation to my father, who I don't talk to as often as I should. He's a perfectly great father, but I've always been more of a Mama's girl. While I know Dad will always be there for me, my mama is my rock.

The tactic works, and I chat with Mama a few more minutes before clicking off and getting ready for bed.

As I wash my face, brush my teeth, and slip into my pajamas, a sinking feeling resonates in my chest.

I might have to forgive Mason Kane tomorrow, but I am not looking forward to it. No one said forgiveness had to be fun.

But hey, if he acts up, I'll have access to plenty of cliffs to shove him off the edge of.

Thinking cheerful thoughts of Mason plummeting off a cliffside, one that's just high enough to where he'll get banged up but won't die, I drift off to sleep.

A FTER A fitful night of sleep knowing I would be spending the next day with Mason, I stand in front of Southern Grace Boutique and Gift Market with my hiking backpack at my feet, a water bottle in my hand, and dressed in olive green workout leggings with a matching sports bra and a loose, white halter-style tank top. I also don an oversized Juniper Grove University sweater at the moment because of the January chill in the air, but once I start the hike and the sun continues to rise, I'll burn alive with the sweater on. Mississippi isn't the best place to experience winter, that's for sure.

I only wore this outfit because it's a good opportunity to snap some pictures for our boutique's social media to advertise our workout gear. I didn't wear it because green is Mason's favorite color, no sir.

Okay. Yeah, whatever. You caught me. I might have decided to forgive, but revenge is still calling my name like a siren's song. I'll show him exactly what he missed out on…

A black Toyota Tundra rolls up and stops in front of me. I can't make out the driver through the tinted windows, but I'm positive this is Mason. He would own a suited up truck like this, lifted to high heaven. Swinging my backpack over one shoulder, I approach the vehicle. Mason walks around the front of the truck and reaches for the passenger door handle. Our hands brush, and that old, electric feeling zings through my body.

I yank my hand away and let Mason open the door for me as he greets me with a shaky "hello" and an unsure smile.

I try my best to offer a smile of reassurance, but the way it feels across my face and watching Mason's smile fall tells me that I managed a grimace over a smile.

Oh, well.

Tossing my water bottle and backpack onto the seat and reaching for the *oh, shoot!* handle, I climb into his truck—literally. I might be taller than your average girl at five-foot-seven, but I still have to climb his truck like I'm scaling Everest.

Once I'm in the seat, my backpack sitting at my feet and water bottle in my lap, Mason softly presses the door closed and jogs around the front to get in on the driver's side. Admittedly, he looks good wearing clothes I've seen him in a million times—black athletic shorts that sit right above his knees and a light gray sweatshirt. His dark brown hair is tucked behind his ears, though a few front strands fall in front of his face. The urge to run my hands through his hair is strong, but I resist.

Barely.

My hand twitches like it's going to act on its own accord, but I grip my water bottle tighter.

"Thanks for agreeing to hike today," Mason says as he clicks his seatbelt on. We meet each other's eyes and a thousand memories and emotions swirl through my thoughts. He clears his throat. "You should put your seatbelt on."

Oh, right. I hastily grab it and buckle myself in.

"Do you hike often?" I ask, trying to make light conversation so this day isn't completely awkward. I already know he wants to apologize, but I'm not going to bring it up. I'll

CHAPTER TWELVE 97

let him do whatever he needs to do whenever he needs to do it. Then I'll accept it and move on. Maybe this will finally allow me to let go of him for good...

"Not really. I've gone on a few when visiting different states, but the tour over the past year has kept me on a pretty tight schedule."

"Ah, yes. How did your tour go? I mean, I saw various news articles stating you had packed out shows and all, but how was it for you?"

He merges onto the interstate, heading south towards the Bluffs. He removes one hand from the wheel and leans against the driver's side window, a reminiscent smile playing at his lips. "It was everything I've dreamed of. The energy while you're on stage is special. I don't think there's a word to describe it other than exhilarating. Hearing thousands of people chanting your name, singing your songs, and having the time of their lives, well, there's nothing like it."

Despite myself, I grin at him. "It truly is everything you wanted, huh? We were hoping that song would get noticed when we recorded it, and..." I drift off, not wanting to speak of what happened when his phone began to blow up with notifications that night in the diner after he drunk-kissed me.

"It comes close," he replies. Then with a sad smile, he glances at me. "I guess I have you to thank for everything."

I don't respond. Instead, I settle in for the two hour ride. Before I realize it, I'm back at Dallas Junction Diner, sitting in a booth, watching Mason shove the swing doors open as he barrels through the exit.

Chapter Thirteen

Karoline - Three Years Ago

A GAINST HIS LIPS, I hiss, "Get off me, Mason!" Using all my strength, I place my hands on his chest and push. The taste of beer mingled with chocolate from his saliva churns my stomach as I grab a napkin and wipe my mouth and tongue off. I take a quick sip of my shake hoping the strawberry flavor will erase the disgusting taste.

Mason, who's now standing at the open end of the table, looks down at me with confusion.

"What, Karoline? I thought you wanted to kiss me."

"I did, but I didn't realize you've been drinking. I should have known by the hollering coming from your place earlier, but..."

"So what?" He cocks an eyebrow.

Fury wafts over me in waves. "What do you mean, 'so what'? I just laid my heart bare for you and you kiss me without saying a word in return. And then I realize you're actually drunk!"

"I'm not drunk," he says, but as if his body wants to tell the truth, he stumbles sideways, placing his hands on the table to steady himself. "Okay, maybe just a little. But it's fine. I do this all the time."

With a snort of disbelief, I stand up to face him. "Yeah, I guess you do, which is why I shouldn't love you, but I guess I have a thing for the bad ones."

He steps closer to me. "Oh, you think you're better than me just because you don't know how to lighten up and have a good time every now and then?"

"I'm eighteen, you idiot!" My fists clench at my side.

He shrugs. "So. I was drinking at eighteen. You just didn't know it."

Rage continues to burn through me.

"Regardless," I hiss through my teeth, "I'm not legal. And even if I were, I wouldn't drink. Look at what it does to you." I gesture my hand down his body.

With a boisterous laugh, he takes another step closer to me, leans down until he's eye level with me, and says, "It makes me a fun night, Vroom."

I shove him away again, and he trips over his feet and falls onto the greasy, tiled floor. Guilt replaces the anger, and I reach a hand down to help him up, but he swats it away and gets up himself. The anger returns as my hand stings from where he knocked it away.

"Mason. You need to go home. Let me walk you out and we can talk about this tomorrow."

"No. Let's talk now, Karoline." His voice rises, and I grab him by the arm to sit him down. He sits, and I move around to the other side of the booth.

"You just said you loved me. You told me a couple weeks ago that any girl would be lucky to have me. I'm trying to give myself to you but you're pushing me away."

I cross my arms. "Because you're drunk, Mason! I don't want you like this."

He laughs with a haughty arrogance. "Well, this is me, baby girl. Take it or leave it."

"I think I'll leave it, thank you very much." I stand, prepared to exit the diner, when he grabs my wrists and tugs me towards him. My side slams into the corner of the table, and I let out a yelp of pain. He lets me go, and I turn around to face him. "What do you think you're doing?"

He snarls, his usual soft, playful features twisting into an expression I've never seen before. "You think you're too good for me, don't you? Well, Vroom, you're not. You're just a kid. I only tried to kiss you because you said you wanted me and I was feeling in the mood. It's not because I like you. It's not because you mean anything to me."

As shock settles in at his words, I find myself frozen in place, unable to move. To my horror, he laughs at me, then his phone begins buzzing like crazy on the table. Picking it up, his eyes widen and his jaw drops open. He hurriedly maneuvers his fingers, swiping and pressing and typing on the screen. "I can't believe this," he whispers. Then he turns to me and stands.

Holding out his phone to me, he scrolls through thousands of social media comments on his "Boyfriend Without Benefits" music video that we'd uploaded the night before.

"And look here," he says, opening up several different emails with requests to represent him and sign him. The screen goes black as he clicks the side button, then he tucks his phone away in his pocket. He reaches for his milkshake on the table and sucks it dry. Then, he drops the glass. It shatters at my feet, the real-life sound of my lively heart stuttering to a stop and splintering.

"Looks like we don't need to talk about anything in the morning, Vroom. I've got better things than you in my future." He smiles sardonically and marches across the diner, barrels through the door, and disappears into the night.

My dress billows around me as it catches a breeze from the closing door. I collapse into the booth and focus on the dust in the window sill as the lights dim around me. The pain in my chest is as if someone reached a hand inside and squeezed my heart. My throat burns as I gasp for a breath that doesn't come. I'm stuck like he hit the pause button on my life when he walked out that door.

I've got better things than you...

Chapter Fourteen

♥

Karoline - Present

A VERSION OF WHO I was died that night.

I sat in that booth all night, staring straight ahead, not moving a muscle. I was numb and shattered all at the same time—the shell of a girl who had walked bravely and confidently into the diner that night ready to confess how she felt. Though I knew there was the possibility he wouldn't reciprocate my feelings, never in a million years did I think he would say the things he said to me that night.

"We're here," Mason says, pulling into a parking spot outside the trailhead leading to the Bluffs.

I awaken from my nightmare, trying to remember the drive here. "Did I…?"

"Yes, you fell asleep. But I figured you needed it if you would let yourself fall asleep in my presence."

That's an understatement. He is the reason I didn't sleep during normal night-time operating hours.

I tilt my head back and forth, stretching my neck out when something falls in my lap.

Mason's sweater.

"Oh, I, uh…" he scratches the back of his neck, "took it off, bundled it up, and placed it between your head and shoulder so that you could have a pillow."

"Thanks."

I give him the sweater, confused at his act of kindness. I guess this is a part of the whole "apology" thing he wants to accomplish today. Whatever the reason, I am grateful to not have a crick in my neck right about now.

Opening the door, I drop out of the truck and reach back in to grab my water bottle, which ended up on the floor by my backpack. I take a sip of water then store the bottle away in the side pocket of the bag before finagling my arms through the loops and securing it tightly to my back. After a little hop to make sure everything is set, I walk to the trailhead, briefly looking back to see if Mason is following.

He is.

"Have you been out here yet?" I ask.

"No, I haven't. But I saw on your social media that you liked to hike here, so I figured it would be a good place to come."

I come to a halt and snap my head around. "You what?"

"Yes, Karoline. I've stalked your socials. It's not just women that do that sort of thing, you know?" He laughs.

"But why?" I demand.

His laughter ceases, and he takes a step towards me.

I back up.

"Because," he steps closer again as I take an equal step back, "I missed you. A lot."

I study his expression. His brown eyes are soft and sad, ghostly. His lips are downturned and his shoulders drooped. Everything about this man, from the tired tone of his voice down to the way he has circles under his eyes, cries that he's in pain.

But why should I care?

He brought my animosity upon himself.

I've got better things than you in my future. The words are like a scratched CD, a haunting repetitive echo from the past.

Without another word, I turn around and start trekking down the short trail again. The path isn't the fun part of coming to the Bluffs. It's the bluffs themselves—red dirt and clay, plenty of opportunities to climb, shade trees to rest under, and random bodies of water to cool off in.

When it's summer, that is.

Mississippi may be warmer than most places in the winter, but it's not warm enough to jump into a lake in January without catching a cold.

We continue to walk in verbal silence, the sounds of rocks and leaves and twigs crunching under our feet with the occasional song of a bird or whisper of the wind through the trees. When we reach the clearing, I take a pause and sip water. Then I shrug my sweater off and stuff it into my backpack.

As I look around to find Mason, I see him standing off in the distance towards the exit of the trail staring at...

Me.

His eyes roam up and down my body, and I don't miss the pink blossoming in his cheeks.

I'm not supposed to care, but I do a celebration dance in my head anyway because my outfit accomplished exactly what I absolutely didn't intend for it to.

Fine. I'll stop trying to lie.

I had hoped my outfit would stop Mason in his tracks today.

"Are you just going to stand there, or…?"

Listen. I tried to detain the smirk playing at my lips, but it escaped, and with it, a smirk's favorite accomplice, a flirty tone.

"When the view's this good, it's worth pausing to admire," Mason flirts back while continuing to slowly peruse my body. I internally scream and chastise myself for cracking the door open. If Mason gets an inch, the man will, in fact, take the whole freaking mile.

"Fine. Suit yourself. I'm heading for the treetop over there." I point across the Bluffs to where a magnolia tree sits on the tallest bluff. One could climb it directly, but I'll be the first to admit that my stamina and arm strength are not that great. Instead, I'll take a zigzag route with a slower incline until I reach the top. All in all, if nothing goes awry, I should make it there in two hours.

I swing my hiking bag back on and start towards my first incline.

"Wait for me!" Mason shouts, but I pick up the pace.

N EARLY THREE HOURS LATER, my hand rests on the textured bark of the massive magnolia tree. It still boasts deep green leaves since it's an evergreen, and it's my favorite tree to come visit during the winter months.

Mason slowed me down big time. Mr. Performer isn't as in shape as he thought he was. But I have to admit, the climb was spectacular, and it was amazing to flex my muscles like this again. The last hike I did was three months ago, and I'd been itching to get back out here, but I have been busy with the store while Hadley was gone and then planning her wedding and finally honeymooning.

"Finally," Mason huffs, collapsing on his butt against the tree. "You do this often?"

"Every few months at least. Typically more than that, yes."

I take in the view while slowing my breathing and heart rate. It's a cloudless day, and the sun is bright overhead. You can see for miles at this top—miles of dirt, trees, lakes, and beautiful nature. I bend down and unzip my bag, stripping my white (now lightly stained with red dirt) tank off and placing it on top of my sweater. Digging in the second section of the bag, I grab my portable ring light stand. I won't need the lighting today, but I do need something to hold the phone while I pose for pictures.

"What are you doing?" Mason asks as I set up the stand.

"I need to snap a few pictures to post to the boutique's socials and website to advertise our athletic wear."

He makes a *hmph* sound, and I dig back in my bag to find my hairbrush and lip gloss. The sheen of sweat coating my face can stay because it'll look intentional for the types of photos I'm taking.

"I could just take your pictures."

I jump at the nearness of Mason's voice and my lip-gloss flies from my hand, bouncing on a rock, and then plummets over the cliffside.

"Dang it, Mason. Don't approach a girl from behind without making your presence known."

"Sorry," he says sheepishly.

"It's fine," I sigh. "I have another tube somewhere in here." I squat down and dig deeper into my bag, looking for the clear gloss. I wanted the soft pink, but no. My favorite tube is probably busted on a rock below somewhere.

"But still. I can take the pictures for you. It'd be easier so you don't have to walk back and forth to adjust angles and such."

Finding the clear gloss, I stand up and face Mason. "It'd probably take longer trying to instruct you on the fine art of photography." I grin at my clever self.

"I'm a famous singer and musician, Vroom. I know how to take and to stage good pictures. Art in all its forms is not lost on me."

My smile fades. Darn it. He's not wrong...

"Fine. You get one chance, and if I don't like it, you leave me be while I do my thing."

He holds out an open hand. "Deal."

With simmering anger surrounding a certain memory of when I held out a hand to him last, I act impulsively, swatting his hand away with the backside of mine. *Man, that felt good.*

"Whatever." I tug my phone from the pocket of my leggings, open the camera, and slap it into his still-open palm.

As I turn my back to him to walk closer to the cliff's edge, he lets out a massive sigh and whispers, "This is going to be tougher than expected."

I choose to ignore the comment and instead search for the perfect photo spot by examining the angle of the sun, the shadows cast by the tree, and, well, where the cliff edge winds and curves because I don't want to end up like my pink lip gloss.

Guilt tugs at my consciousness for smacking his hand away. It's hard to reconcile the guilt to the empowering feeling of the action, so I conclude it's best not to dwell too much on it right now. I brush through my hair and swipe gloss over my lips, then set the items out of view.

Picking out a spot, I direct Mason where to stand and the angle to capture the picture from. He does so without complaint or comment, but when I move to go view the picture, he holds up a hand.

"Wait. Let me stage one real quick."

"I—"

"Before you protest, just let me do this one picture, okay?"

I grit my teeth. "Fine."

He instructs me to squat down, resting an elbow lazily on my outer knee while I shift all my weight to the outstretched leg. He tells me to place my other arm up as if I'm running my fingers through my hair.

"Don't smile," he says, then he lays on his stomach, turning my phone upside down into the burgundy sand. "Karoline, stop looking at me with confusion written all over your face. Look away from the camera, don't smile, and think fierce thoughts. Think about what it would be like to sock me in the jaw or toss me over a cliff, okay?"

Despite myself, I spit laughter. The motion throws me off balance, and I hit my butt with an "oof" then roll on my side.

Within a moment, Mason stands above me, dirt coating the front of his light gray t-shirt, with his hand once again outstretched.

My laughter dies and guilt tugs at my heart again. This time, I take his hand, and he pulls me to my feet.

"See? That wasn't so bad, was it?" He smirks, and the guilt disappears.

"I have multiple incurable diseases now, I'm sure." I wipe my hand down on the back of my leggings for show. He laughs and shakes his head, amused, and I turn my back to him.

He laughs harder. "No, but your backside matches that imprint in the ground. And that red dirt looks real nice against your olive green. It's like you're my belated Christmas present."

Heat floods my neck, and after running my feet through a dirt imprint that does resemble my bottom, I face Mason again. "Stop looking at my butt!"

"You turned around. Of course I took my chance to look." He shrugs with a familiar, boyish grin and spark in his eyes. It's an expression I've seen a thousand times, an expression I once fell in love with. "Oh, and Karoline? Is that a heart-shaped peppermint tattooed at the base of your neck?"

I finger the tattoo I got for my eighteenth birthday because I knew we would always be together, at least as friends. What a stupid mistake...

A flood of emotion overwhelms me and I stand frozen, staring at the man who was once my very best friend and confidant. A man I could freely be myself around without fear of judgment or complaint. I once would have shaken my butt in his face for making such a comment because I knew he wasn't laughing *at* me but *with* me.

What has he turned me into? Some self-conscious, shallow version of myself who feels like she has to be perfect in order to win his approval? A girl who can't even take a joke for fear that she's not measuring up somehow? Then that begs the question why I even want his approval and why I want to measure up to him.

But I know the answer to that...

It's because the feeling of love never went away, it was only hidden by deep cuts and wounds. The hate I have for Mason is simply scar tissue covering the source of the internal wound.

I still love Mason Kane, and that's why I can't fully heal. Loving him is a double-edge sword, piercing straight through my bones and marrow and shattering my soul.

"Karoline?"

Traces of concern fill his voice, and when I meet his gaze, a single tear breaks free of its prison and rolls down my cheek.

"Karoline… It's time we talked about what happened."

I only nod, still fighting tears threatening to fall. He leads me to the base of the magnolia and we sit down facing each other.

"This is like old times, isn't it?" he says, looking up at the tree.

I sniffle. "Just say whatever you need to say, Mason."

He takes a deep breath, then begins. "I'm sorry. And I need you to know that I truly mean those words. Kissing you that night while I was drunk was a mistake I never intended to make. And then to say what I said to you? Man, Karoline…" He runs a hand through his hair. "You have no idea how those words have haunted me."

"I think I do," I bite. "Imagine being on the receiving end."

"I know. You're right. They should have haunted me, but I am so sorry they've been your ghosts, too. I never should have said those things, and I can say I honestly didn't mean any of it. I could give you all the reasons they flew unbidden from my mouth, but at the end of the day, there is no excuse good enough to justify it. Karoline, I was an idiot."

Mason sniffs, tears beginning to tread lightly down his face. My heart stutters at the sight, and I know he's truly sorry. I've known it since I first heard his song "Midnight Mistakes." I know I have to forgive him.

"Karoline, I can't believe I did that to you. I knew you liked me, it wasn't hard to tell. And I was fighting attraction to you all summer long. So when you confessed to me, it felt like I could freely give in. But that was the alcohol talking, and I was still butt-hurt over Cassidy's rejection. You were there, looking very pretty, and saying things that inflated my ego with each syllable out of your mouth.

"Every time I thought that I could possibly date you or be with you over that summer, I cut it off. You deserved better. You still deserve better. You are one heck of a woman, and you always have been. You're sweet, kind, and gentle, but you're also not a pushover and know how to fight and stand up for yourself, which I have always admired about you. Karoline," he rubs his eyes, "I am so sorry for making you think anything less of yourself by my reckless, thoughtless words and actions that night. The kiss... That was real. I'm a natural flirt, and all summer, with each passing day we spent together, I became curious as to how you would taste. But that wasn't how I was ever supposed to find out."

I sit there, tears freely falling from my face as I soak in his words. I believe him, but I still have one burning question. "Why did you leave for Nashville the next day and never bother to call or text or stop by or reach out or anything? You just left, Mason." As I speak those last words, sobs shake my body, and I collapse against the tree. Mason's arm wraps around my shoulder and he tugs me closely against his chest, using his other hand to run his fingers from my scalp down my tresses.

"I left without saying a word because I was a terrified, selfish, egotistical prick who didn't have the guts to face you, the one woman I swore I'd never date because I didn't want to end up hurting you. I couldn't tell you in person, so I wrote you that song. I'm so sorry, Karoline. Please, find it in your heart to forgive me."

His fingers continue to caress me, and I allow myself a moment to enjoy his touch and his closeness.

But only for a moment.

I pull away and wipe my eyes, thankful my eyelashes are long and dark enough that mascara isn't a daily need for me. "I accept your apology, Mason. I forgive you. But just know that it doesn't change anything. I don't trust you, and I still have a lot of emotions to work through regarding that night. I have been living with them stuffed in a box labeled 'do not touch, will detonate' since I collected my wits and walked out of that diner the next morning."

"You spent the night there?" His eyes blaze with torturous pain.

"Yes. I was stuck. Frozen. I couldn't move. Everyone around me was in motion but on my end, time had stopped. You hurt me, Mason."

"I'm so—"

"Don't. You don't have to keep apologizing. I appreciate your candor and sensitivity, and now it's time we both move forward. What do you say?"

I stand up and Mason follows suit.

Shakily and slowly, I reach out my hand to him. He takes it and holds tight. No shake takes place, but the deal is satisfied.

"Okay," I sniff and wipe away any remaining tears rolling down my cheeks. "I think photos are now a hopeless pursuit due to my red, puffy face. Why don't we start heading back?"

"Sounds good, and I did get some pictures. Look them over," he says as he digs into his backpack. "And here, I brought these for you."

Mason tosses me a value size pack of Boston Style peanuts, and I catch them with one hand.

"I see you still have your softball reflexes," he compliments. I grin and tear the package open, tossing a red candy-coated peanut into my mouth.

"Yep. I still play rec ball every spring, Peppermint."

We both pause at my using of his nickname in a casual tone, and instead of backtracking or trying to fight the moving on, I roll with it and shrug. If I'm putting the past in the past, I might as well start now.

Mason grins like a fool.

"Let's get out of here." I roll my eyes, sling my backpack over my shoulder, and start the trek back.

"I'll follow your lead," he says.

"Don't stare at my backside. We can't attempt to be friends again if you go lusting after me."

Behind me, he snickers. "I'm not making promises I can't keep anymore, Vroom."

I glance back at him just in time to see him trip over a tree root, face plant on the ground, and then roll a few times in my direction. He groans but sits up before I can make it to him. He grins sheepishly at me and shakes his head, red dirt flying in all directions. Unable to control my laughter, I double over, pretty sure I'm in the process of creating new abs.

Wiping a joyful tear from my eye, I watch as he climbs to his feet and shrugs. "Karma has your back, Karoline Wright."

Chapter Fifteen

Mason - Present

I TRIED TO REFRAIN from flirting.

That's a lie. I gave about thirty percent of my effort. But don't worry.

God put me in my place.

That woman lights a fire in me that brings out my best and worst traits. How did I not notice that back at twenty-one, or at the very least, on my birthday that fateful night? It's been four dreadful days since I last saw Karoline in person. My agent, Rob, came down the day after Karoline and I went hiking because he found out about the commercial and promo ads I was doing with the boutique.

Needless to say, he was not happy about me keeping him in the dark in the name of "just resting and recuperating" here in Mississippi.

"Let me look over the contract one more time," Rob grunts, placing his reading glasses on his nose, reaching for the stack of papers across from him. He sits on a barstool at the island counter while I sit on the other side, plucking at the strings on my custom cherry-red Taylor 814ce guitar while I listen for a tune to fit special lyrics I've been writing down.

Rob's nonsense about the contract has been going on for the past two days. I'm set to meet with Karoline and Genevieve today at the boutique, and Rob is insistent about tagging along and making sure I'm getting good exposure and pay. But I keep telling him I'm not doing this promotion for exposure or pay…

I'm doing it for Braxton as a thank you, at least that's what I've told everyone.

The reality? I'm doing it to get my foot in the door with Karoline's good graces again. To me, that's more important than money or fame.

Three years too late to realize that, bud, I chastise myself. A melody begins to play in my head, a sound of renewed hope, joy, and surprises. I transfer the sound from my head to the guitar.

"Mason, I'm telling you. You need to demand more pay for this promotion." He removes his glasses from his face and sets them on top of the papers. "The woman will get ladies and gentlemen flocking to not only her brick and mortar store, but also her online community because you're a part of it."

"I've told you before. This isn't about pay. It's why I didn't want to bother you with it."

"Look, kid."

"I'm not a kid," I growl.

"Okay, okay." He holds his hands up. "But you are a brand. You have to treat yourself as such."

"I do. All the time. It's good to do things for others, though. And this is one thing that I want to do for my friends. God allowed me to meet Braxton at the right place and the right time, and I want to act on my thankfulness for His timing."

"I can't talk you out of this, can I?" Rob asks, defeat lacing his voice.

"Afraid not," I say. Rob's downcast look tugs at my heart, though. "However, if you would like to come alongside me and be a part of it, I would be appreciative. Your wisdom and insight are always welcomed, even if I choose a different direction."

Rob perks up. "Glad to hear it, Mason. What time is the meeting again?"

I set my guitar down, satisfied with the melody, and I check my silver watch. "In about thirty minutes, actually. So we should get going."

"Lead the way," Rob says, gesturing towards the front door of the cabin. We step out, walk through the deadened January grass, and hop into my Tundra.

Fifteen minutes later, we arrive at the boutique a little over two hours before it's set to open. I tug on the door, but it's locked. Before I even get the chance to knock, Hadley waltzes up, twists a knob, and holds the door open for us.

"Sorry about that. You guys are a little early."

"Is that okay?" I ask, though I'm already pushing my way through the door in search of Karoline.

"Fine by me!" Hadley grins and Rob introduces himself. I guess I should have made introductions, as that is the polite southern thing to do, but my eyes are scanning the building for Karoline like I'm the Secret Service on watch for an assassination attempt. Where is that beautiful woman?

I search by the clothing racks, then by the jewelry section. I examine the candles, the knick-knack gifts, the shoes. I even take a quick stroll through the lingerie portion of the store, careful not to let my eyes linger too long on pieces of silk or lace. I know *exactly* where my mind would drift to. In fact, it does as I come across this silky olive green tank and shorst set that would look plain sexy on...

"Whatcha doing?"

"Karoline!" A smile sweeps my face as she pokes her head out of a door that leads to what I presume to be the back of the store meant for employees only.

"I don't think that's your size, but I can see what we have in the back if you'd like."

My eyes widen with horror as I realize I'm clutching the silky shorts. I mask the embarrassment with what I do best. Easing into a lazy grin, I reply, "You know, I was just thinking that I could buy this for *you*. As a Valentine's Day gift and all. A way to say thank you for including me in your promotion."

She narrows her blue eyes as she steps from behind the door and saunters towards me. "I will *not* wear that for you, Mason Kane. Plus, I don't do Valentine's Day. It's a beacon for single awareness. Not a fan."

Unable to control myself, I take two steps towards Karoline, backing her up against the white bricked wall. I place a hand beside her head and lean in as she tilts her chin up, eyes blazing.

She still smells like lavender.

"I never said you had to wear it for me, but if that's what you want to do, Vroom, by all means, be my guest. I'll help you celebrate Valentine's Day in any shape or form you want. Maybe you'll appreciate the holiday as a fun celebration of love after that."

I fully expect her to shove me away when she places a firm hand on my chest, but instead, she stands on her tiptoes, our lips mere breaths away from each other. "Oh, please. You couldn't handle me in that silk, anyway."

Then she steps around me, leaving me with a slack jaw and thoughts that I'm going to have to repent for.

"What's going on over here?" Hadley asks, her eyes shifting from me to Karoline, a twinge of suspicion carrying through her voice.

"Nothing!" we both shout.

"Okay, well, Genevieve and Presley will be here soon and we can get this meeting started," Hadley says, walking into the back room. Rob follows after her, throwing a narrow-eyed glance at me. Apparently, Hadley wasn't the only one to witness me backing Karoline against the wall like we were the only two people in this building.

I glance at Karoline, who's wearing a smug expression like she got one over on me, which admittedly, I didn't expect her response, but I appreciated the confidence she exuded.

On the hike, she seemed unsure of herself, unsure of how to interact with me now. I'm glad to see she's getting back to the girl I used to know.

We follow Hadley and Rob to the back. We all take a seat on fold-out chairs at a fold-out plastic table. The door opens, and Hadley bounces out to greet Genevieve and her agent.

The three of them enter the back room. Genevieve waves at me with both hands and wrists full of bangles clacking together, wearing ripped jeans, a tassel crop top, and hooped earrings that are almost as big as her elongated face. Her makeup is heavy, making her look like a gypsy princess.

She sits next to me, her agent, Presley, sitting on her other side. Rob, Hadley, and Karoline sit across from us, Karoline directly across from me, her eyes flicking between me and Genevieve.

"It's good to see you again," Genevieve says.

"You too, Gen." I smile at my friend who has helped me navigate this world over the past few years. I knew she'd help me with this promotion without asking for much. She's always been a big supporter of me and my work as I have been for her.

"All right, everyone. I believe we all know each other," Hadley says then turns to face Karoline. "Well, except Karoline. Karoline, this is Genevieve Rhodes and her agent, Presley Saint."

Karoline smiles softly, standing up and reaching a hand diagonally to shake first Genevieve's hand, then Presley's. "It's nice to meet y'all."

"The pleasure is mine." Genevieve turns to Hadley. "Thank you so much for allowing me to be a part of this huge moment for your store and jewelry line. I hope our names can drum up a lot of business and success for you."

"We are grateful! I'm going to turn this meeting over to the spearhead of the campaign, Karoline Wright."

All eyes lock in on the pretty girl sitting in front of me wearing black leggings and a chunky maroon sweater dress, a color that brings out the warmth in her tanned skin.

She nervously twiddles her fingers then smiles tentatively.

"Thanks for meeting today, guys. We are going to begin filming tomorrow…"

As Karoline goes over all the details of the promotional video and different ads that we are going to do, I get lost in the animated way she talks about her marketing plan. She truly loves this job. It shows in her bright eyes, half-moon smile, and the way she leans forward, her focus attentively attune to every person she speaks with.

She's grown so much over the past three years. Karoline exudes confidence, grace, and a fiery passion that is so. freaking. attractive. Man, I was such a douche for doing what I did to her… If I would have been mature, sober, and the man she thought she loved, Karoline and I could be a thing right now. We could possibly be married, maybe with a little Karoline or Mason on the way…

"Mason?" Genevieve places a hand on my knee then leans in to whisper against my ear. "Everything okay? You look like someone stole your favorite guitar. I thought your text said everything was good between the two of you now."

I place a hand over hers and squeeze. She's always been in my corner, calming me down when I get nervous or anxious, listening to me drone on and about Karoline…

"I'm okay. Just thinking about what a tool I was in my past."

She chuckles, leaning away.

I glance at Karoline, who is still talking, but the way she flicks her eyes from Genevieve to me screams that she thinks something's going on between us. I make a note to correct that assumption as soon as possible. Though Karoline says she forgives me, she made it clear she didn't trust me, and I have every intention to change that.

This woman is not going to get away from me.

Better yet, I'm not going to screw up again. At least I'm going to try like heck not to.

The meeting eventually draws to a close, and we all go our separate ways. Karoline continually side-eyed me and scrutinized every interaction me and Genevieve had.

When Rob and I drive back to the house, he asks to go see the progress on the home I'm building down the road, so I oblige him, hoping after this I can shake him and go find Karoline to make sure the air is clear between us.

As we roll up to the house under construction, my phone buzzes, and I reach in my back pocket to grab it.

> **Vroom:** Here is the itinerary for the filming of the commercial. Let me know if you have any questions.

I glance at the papers tucked in my visor. One paper in that stack is the same itinerary Karoline just sent me, and I smile to myself.

Well, fellas. Looks like Karoline Wright went hunting for and found a reason to text me.

Chapter Sixteen

♥

Karoline - Present

I READ THE MESSAGE again. He responded to me three days later, and I don't know what to make of this. I found myself checking my phone while in class, while arranging displays at work, while showering… Basically, every buzz sent my fragile heart into a tizzy at the thought of Mason's name on my phone. Yes, his contact name finally made it to his actual name.

> **Mason:** Actually, I do have a few questions. Can we meet to talk about them in person? 7pm at the movie theater?

That sly man. Every fiber of my being wants to sit in a darkened theater with him…

> **Me:** How are we going to talk while watching a movie?

> **Mason:** Who said anything about talking during the movie? We can talk before or after. Grab dinner?

"Oooh, who are you smiling at like that?" Chanel asks, and I school my face back into a blank neutrality.

"No one. I'm not smiling at anyone."

She slides up next to me, and I click my screen black.

"Whatcha hiding me from me, Kar?" Chanel bumps my hip with hers in her leggings and baggy sweatshirt. I match her appearance currently, but it looks like I'm going to be changing soon.

"It's nothing. Mason just wants to meet up to discuss some questions he has about the promotional video that we're shooting tomorrow."

She wiggles her brows and starts making kissing noises. I've kept her up to date with everything regarding him, and she has solidly entered the camp of "the famous country star has returned for his long lost lover."

"It's not like that!" I holler, turning my back to her to pour a glass of water. My kitchen is small, very similar to the twins' kitchen above me.

"The lady doth protest too much."

I take a sip of water to cool the flame burning through my skin at the thought of sitting through a movie with Mason. "Fine. He invited me to go see a movie under the guise of needing questions answered." I mean, it was obvious. Which makes me wonder if he saw through my text about the itinerary to begin with? I *am* the one who handed him the paper copy before he left the boutique a few days ago.

My days since I've last seen him have been excruciatingly monotonous as I awaited a message from him. I worked the morning shift, then went to my afternoon classes. I ended my days studying with Chanel, which is what I'm currently doing.

Or was.

I think back to the simple message I sent him. I just *had* to break my "don't message first rule" and text Mason after our meeting because...

Fine. I'll be honest. I texted him because seeing him with Genevieve got under my skin. I thought maybe if I caved and sent a message first then he would continue a conversation with me.

But no. Silence for a few days ensued. It sent my brain spiraling down a rabbit hole of thoughts and questions and research.

I have spent most of my class time googling the two of them, analyzing their photos, the interviews they've had, etc., looking for any indication of a relationship. I don't think they have one judging by the way Mason continues to hit on me every chance he gets, but you never know...

There was radio silence for the past three days, after all.

Not that I care. He doesn't have to text me.

I'm *fine.*

He apologized and I have forgiven him, but I haven't forgotten what he's capable of. And remembering that should quiet the stupid thoughts swirling in my head, desperately trying to kickstart my heart into chasing after his affection.

"Are you going to go?" Chanel asks, saddling up next to me at the kitchen table. "He apologized the other day. You said you forgave him. And for what it's worth, by what you've told me, he seems sincere. Maybe it's okay to give him the space to prove himself to you?"

I toss her words around, testing them out on my tongue. "Prove himself? What's there to prove? He's back to flirting with me, which signifies that he hasn't lost the cocky, arrogant side of him. Who's to say I won't hurt his fragile pride again and elicit a venomous response from him?"

"No one can promise you that he won't, Kar. But you'll never know if you don't give him the space to show you who he is now. We both know you're still in love with the man." She tucks a strand of auburn hair behind her ear and gives me a look that reminds me of her mother offering sage advice.

Air fills my cheeks before I breathe it out. "But just because I have lingering feelings doesn't mean that I can date him suddenly. He's a famous country star now, Channel." I picture myself on a stage in a darkened arena, the sole spotlight beaming down on me as I cry hot mascara tears and clutch my chest, gasping for breath. "I don't want a spotlight on me when he rips my heart out again."

"Who's to say he's going to do that again? Everyone deserves a second chance to make up for their past mistakes." She pauses. "I know you're hurt. I know an apology from him doesn't magically wash away the sins of the past. But Karoline, you know the whole family thought you two would end up together. You two work together, and you do it well. You keep his ego in check and he inflates yours. It's a win-win." Chanel laughs with a shrug. I shake my head, laughing with her. Only she would think two people were good together because of an ego balance.

She continues. "But really, the two of you work because you know each other. The good, the bad, and the ugly. And accepting those things about each other, which the two of you have done your entire lives, creates a solid foundation."

I don't think I would call where we left off a few years ago a solid foundation, but that doesn't matter anyway.

"I hate it when you're right." I playfully shove against her. "But only about giving him space to prove who he is today. I'm still not dating him. *This isn't a date.* It's two old friends catching up and two temporary coworkers talking business. That's all."

She gives me a toothy grin and wraps an arm around my shoulder, scooching so close she's almost sitting on my lap. "Sounds good, Kar. But we have one more thing to figure out…"

"Hm?"

Chanel abruptly stands up and pulls me by the arm. "What you're going to wear!"

"Jeans and a baggy sweater," I whine as she drags me to my bedroom. I stumble along after her to keep my shoulder socket intact.

Once we're in front of my door, she stops and spins around to face me. "No ma'am. I'm hoping this won't be the case, but if you're spotted out with *the* Mason Kane tonight, your pretty face will be all over the tabloids in the morning. You are not wearing your baggy sweater. Period."

"You're two for two today," I jest, then I allow her to drag me into my room and dress me up like I'm her favorite doll.

While she's combing through my closet looking for sparkles or tassel—*maybe both,* I think with a cringe—I shoot a text to Mason letting him know to pick me up…

From my apartment.

Maybe I really am losing my mind.

Once I've slipped into a fitted black, sparkly, long-sleeve dress, Chanel pins my hair into an over-one-shoulder look and picks out red jewelry to accompany the black. After covering my face in makeup—a smoky eye with a bold, blood-red lip—she places my red stiletto booties at my feet.

"This is where I draw the line, Chanel." I stare at the seductive heels. Not only are they four inches, but they have heart cutouts along the outer sides. "This is a friendly outing to Grove Cinemas, not a red carpet debut. I'm only wearing this dress and hair style because I happen to like fashion. And you're unfortunately right about what would happen if we were photographed by some happenstance tonight."

"Eh, to be honest, I had an inkling you might veto the heels. But you do need to wear these bad boys out on the town one day. Here," she digs around in my closet, "wear these."

Chanel replaces the heels with a pair of fresh white sneakers.

I grin. "Now that's more like it. Cute but still classy."

My phone vibrates on the vanity as I'm slipping into my shoes. When I get the last one tied, I check it.

BREAKING NEWS:

Darcy Marshall is sworn in as the 47th President of the United States. Click <u>here</u> to watch a recap of the Inauguration.

I don't get into politics much, but Darcy Marshall was the best candidate for the job. I don't regret voting for him, and I was thrilled when they announced he won. Also, his wife? She's adorable. They look so cute together on the screen. I wonder how they navigate the spotlight?

If I date Mason, will I be thrust into the spotlight?

Of course I would...

The real question is, can I handle that?

My phone buzzes in my hand again.

> **Mason:** On my way. See you in fifteen minutes.

I don't respond. Instead, I focus on identifying the emotions swirling within me.

A twinge of uncertainty about tonight. Excitement. A bit scared. Defensive. Hopeful...

How can a person experience all these contradicting emotions at once and survive?

"Channel. I'm scared." I fight back tears, unsure of which emotion to accredit them to. I only know that I never want to feel as unwanted as I felt sitting in that corner booth three years ago.

My cousin wraps me in a hug. I squeeze my phone as I bring my arms up to pull her closer, needing the warmth and comfort of her presence.

"I know, I know," she coos, careful not to run her hands through my styled hair. "That's okay. It's okay to be scared. It would be weird if you weren't. But I'm proud of you." She releases me and grabs my free hand with both of hers. I use the back of the hand grasping my phone to blot my cheeks.

"For what? Probably making a fool of myself again with Mason?"

Chanel tightens her grip on my hand. "No. For being brave and choosing not to let the past continue to stifle your shine. Look at you." She gestures towards the full-length mirror by my vanity.

I look at the woman in the mirror. *She's breathtaking,* I admit, on the verge of sounding as conceited as Mason. From the sneakers to the sparkling dress that sits mid-thigh, to the sultry makeup and Hollywood-ready hair.

I'm not eighteen-year-old Karoline anymore. I'm not the woman he left in that diner.

I'm twenty-one, twenty-two come March.

I'm a woman, doing a job I love, surrounded by people I love, in a town I've grown to love.

Chanel is right. No matter what happens tonight or going forward, I'm not stuck in the past. I'm free to choose to offer a second chance to Mason, and I'm free to choose to not to.

The decision is mine and mine alone.

Chapter Seventeen

♥

Karoline - One Year Ago

M Y WORST NIGHTMARE FOLLOWS me into the land of the living.

I stare at the billboards along the highway, promoting an upcoming concert on the coast of Mississippi at the Coliseum. His face appears on every other sign, a head full of dark brown hair that contrasts perfectly against his light but tanned skin. The image is blown up so big that I can pinpoint exactly where the golden ring around his dark brown irises should be.

At least I could if I wasn't going eighty down the interstate.

To torture me further, it's at the moment the song changes on the radio, a new single by the year's hottest country artist, Mason Kane. A soft thrum of a guitar filters through the sound system in my car, and after a brief interlude, his deep, smooth voice drowns out the sound of the road beneath my tires.

Though I grip the steering wheel as if it's my lifeline and I scowl at the radio for playing this song, I'm too far gone to pretend I wasn't listening to the radio in hopes the song would come on at random. Nor can I hide the fact that I took this drive just to see his face. If I plugged my phone in and intentionally chose the song or if I googled pictures of him to look at, then I would have to confess to being some variant of a masochist.

But when his music plays by random chance and his face is somewhere I can't avoid looking because it's along my route to the beach, then I have excuses to point to as to why I'm a haunted soul at the moment.

As his lyrics invade my senses, chilling me to my bones as it does every time I hear this song, I'm forced to relive one of the worst nights of my existence. Mason sings about a diner, a drunken kiss, and his biggest regret.

The song is packed full of emotion, and I'm not naïve enough to miss that this is a very public apology to a very private thing he did to me.

How could he make this song public? He could have sent the lyrics to me. Or a private video. Or—here's a winner—picked up his freaking phone, invited me out, and apologized to me in person!

But no.

He's Mason Kane.

He has to make money off my pain.

And yet here I am, on the prowl to scoop an additional helping of pain and self-loathing onto my plate because I'm pulling into the Coliseum parking lot, clutching a ticket to my demise.

It's me. Hi. I *am* some variant of masochist. When I said I took this drive to see his face, it wasn't just on a billboard.

Therapy. That's where I should have gone.

After maneuvering my way through the crowded parking lot on the hunt for a spot, I find one in the back row of the lot, then grimace at the heeled, bedazzled pink cowgirl boots my feet are strutting. While adorable, they're not practical. Yet, I chose to wear them to stand for hours on end along with a matching pink halter top dress with tassels.

The things women do for fashion…

And to satisfy their toxic desires.

Groups of women who are showing up late like me flock towards the coliseum in a variety of attire. Some are chic country like me while others are redneck country in jeans and a t-shirt. I even see a few women sporting "I heart Mason" shirts.

I want to punch them.

Only to knock sense into them, not because I'm jealous or anything.

"Why are you even here, Karoline?" I ask under my breath. My brain searches for a valid answer, a perfect excuse. A justifiable reason to walk through those coliseum gates up ahead.

But I have none.

The sad, sick reality is that I miss the man who said he has better things than me in his future. He wasn't wrong; I'm shamefully walking into a sold-out show of his.

Why can't I let him go? Why am I taking a knife to my own throat?

If I could just get his attention… if I could make him see me. Maybe he'd regret not choosing me. Maybe, just maybe, he'd come running back to me.

If he saw me, would he say the one thing I've been waiting a lifetime for him to say? If he told me he loved me, would I say it back?

The coastal Mississippi July air is stifling and wet, like I'm standing in a sauna. A slight breeze bristles through the palm trees, picking up strands of my hair and disposing of them right into my newly applied pink gloss coating my lips. After spitting the hair out of my mouth and tugging the fine threads off my lips, my gaze latches onto the front gates.

Next step…

Walk through the gates.

Stepping over the threshold, handing my ticket over, and going through security feels like selling my soul to the devil. The music that was playing stops and applause erupts through the crowds inside the building. The opening act must be taking the stage. I purposefully timed my arrival so that I would get here after the masses had stormed the building, though there are other stragglers like me finding their way to their seats.

The opening act performs while I climb my way into the first row of seats, directly in front of the stage. Mason wouldn't be able to pick me out in the crowd here as there is a sea of super fans flooding the floor between me and the stage.

But I would be able to see him.

The opener continues his setlist, and I sit in my seat, enjoying the atmosphere around me. But then he finishes, and before I know it, Mason is strutting onto the stage with his cherry-red guitar strapped around his back. Man, oh man… he looks *good.*

He is wearing ripped jeans and a tight white t-shirt, and with his thick, chocolate hair styled back, he's got a James Dean vibe going on. He's just missing the leather jacket, but I can't blame him for choosing to ditch that in this heat.

What am I doing?

The crowd thunders around me, everyone jumping to their feet as he swings his guitar around and begins strumming chords, crafting a sweet melody with a twinge of rock blended seamlessly into country. As his voice carries through the speakers and the sound waves tickle my ears, I'm transported to days spent under the shade tree and nights in his room, painting while he strummed and wrote music.

An ache blossoms in my chest, spreading its poison throughout my veins, rendering me immobile and unable to take my eyes off the human I once considered my closest friend and love of my life.

He dominates the stage and captivates the audience. A natural. He was born to do this.

Maybe he was right two years ago when he said he had better things ahead than me. If he would have returned my feelings in a proper manner and never uttered the words aimed to kill, would he be on this stage tonight?

I guess we will never know because at the end of the day, he said what he said.

Why am I here?

Mason's song ends and it blends into another upbeat tune. He tantalizes the crowd by tugging at the hem of his shirt and lifting it to wipe sweat from his brow. The camera zooms in on his bare skin, and his abs are projected onto the screen behind him for all the world to see...

Friends, there's a whole set of eight abs present. Turns out God was just waiting for the right time to make Mason Kane physically perfect.

Karoline, stop ogling him. Remember what he did!

When that song comes to an end, Mason introduces himself, thanking everyone for coming out tonight to have a good time with him. Then, he launches into a cover song of "Starting Over" by Chris Stapleton. As he sings about taking chances and hard roads, I wonder if he ever thinks of me the way I ruminate over him each and every day. Does he remember the words he said to me? Does he remember kissing me? Does guilt chew him up alive when he thinks about that night?

Or am I a stain on his past? A blot in need of removal? Was writing that apology song his way of clearing his own conscience while not having to confront me? Was it his way of taking a Tide To-Go pen to our ruined history?

That thought sends my stomach into knots of uneasiness and fury, and before I know it, the very song occupying my thoughts begins to play through speakers. As Mason strums the chords, he steps up to the mic and says, "Midnights are the hardest. It's when my darkest demons come to haunt and play, reminding me of countless mistakes I've made in my life. You've all related to this new song, and I'm excited to play it for the first time ever for y'all tonight."

Then he launches into "Midnight Mistakes" and I finally realize exactly what I'm doing at this concert: hoping and praying he will see me, stop the show, part the crowd to run to me, drop to his knees, beg for forgiveness, cry tears of sorrow, then sweep me up into a kiss that I know should have been our first one.

But Mason Kane can't see me.

He has no idea I'm here.

And I'm only stabbing myself over and over with a thousand needles with every breath I take inside this hellish coliseum.

Forcing myself to stand, I push through the crowd on shaky, wobbly knees and fight to constrain the burning tears of disgust at my pathetic, deprecating, self-sabotaging actions I took by coming here this evening. Once I reach my car, turn on the AC, slide in, and slam the door shut, the deluge pours from my eyes.

I hate myself.

How did I get here? Driving six hours to put myself through utter misery for the sake of feeling something again?

What kind of pathetic shell of a woman have I become?

Why do I allow him to have this control over me?

When will I *just. let. go…?*

Chapter Eighteen

♥

Mason - Present

"**H**AVE I TOLD YOU how stunning you look tonight?" I whisper in Karoline's ear as the ads play on the big screen. No one else is in the theater, as I booked the entire room out for just the two of us. I didn't tell Karoline that, and she hasn't inquired about us being the only two in here tonight.

Karoline rolls her eyes, but I don't miss the pink flush in her cheeks. "Only a million times. You can stop feeding my ego now."

"That's where you're wrong, *Little Ma'am.* I'll feed your ego as long as you'll let me. My compliments are like a faucet that's stuck on... I'll continue to pour them out until you're overflowing with confidence."

She laughs, and it's a sound I never want to be separated from again. "That was the cheesiest thing I've ever heard you say, Peppermint. For the love of all things good and holy, do *not* say something like that again."

With a snicker, I settle back into the reclining chair. I, for one, am glad theaters have been remodeled to hold these comfy chairs. Those fold-down ones that squeaked with every weight shift were anxiety-inducing. Though, these bulkier ones make it more difficult to scoot close to your date and snuggle up.

Karoline would say this isn't a date, but I know better.

I glance at her out of the corner of my eye. She's fiddling with her fingers on her lap and biting the bottom of her red lips. Signature nervous energy *courtesy of Karoline.*

This is a date.

My first one with Karoline Wright.

And, God-willing, my last first date ever.

She turns her head in my direction, and I don't bother to look away. Yeah, she caught me staring, and with the lights dimming around us, she's about to catch me leaning in…

"N-no," Karoline stammers at the last minute, turning her head so that my lips crash against her cheek. "Uh…"

I ease out of her space. "Well, this is awkward."

While I let out a long breath, she pats her cheek with the back of her hand.

We both sit facing forward, the awkwardness of the situation rolling over us in waves. At least, I think she feels it by the way she won't look at me.

I might be a reformed player of sorts, but my impulsivity and lack of patience is still sorely intact. Staring straight ahead at previews playing on the screen, though I couldn't tell you what they were about, I blurt, "Wanna clue me in,

Vroom? I thought things were finally defrosting between us."

Beside me, Karoline sniffles, and I turn my attention towards her as the big screen darkens. It's hard to see her expression clearly in the soft glow of the dim lights around the theater. But then, the screen in front of us lights up, and the pain and confusion written on her face ties my stomach into knots.

"I'm sorry I tried to kiss you." No excuses. Just an apology. I have once again broken my self-made vow to let Karoline set the pace of whatever is going on between us.

She sniffles again and presses underneath her eyes with the tip of her index finger. "It's okay. I just... Mason, I can't let myself love you again. It's easier to keep the walls up. It's easier to continue to hold your head to the flames for what you did. It's easier to believe that you couldn't possibly change."

Karoline trails off, tears running down her face. I'm stunned silent by her confession because reading into the gray lines of her words, Karoline is screaming that she still loves me. And it seems like she never stopped. How in the world am I supposed to be patient and let her come back around to me when I know she's already there? When I know she's refusing to believe me because of the fear locking up her heart?

She shifts her gaze to the screen, which is now showing the opening scene of the comedic action movie we came to watch. "It hurts too much to love you. Just... just let me keep the chains around my heart."

Without thinking, I lift my fingers to her chin and turn her head towards me. She gasps but doesn't try to free herself from my grip. Pegging her with sincerity in my eyes, I whisper, "You can guard yourself for now, Karoline, but I won't let you do that for much longer. Just so you're aware of my plans, I'm going to bring a wrecking ball to your walls and a key chiseled to fit the chain locks around your heart. I'm not worthy of your love, but Karoline, I'm selfish enough to admit I need it." I drop my hand and face the film.

We spend the rest of the two-hour long movie in silence, our shoulders inches apart; the heat radiating off her skin mixes with my own, creating a livewire connection that almost has my hair standing on its end. Every glance in Karoline's direction reveals a woman who is fighting her feelings harder than a soldier on the frontlines of war.

I just want to free her from that battle.

But I have to practice patience... something I've never been good at.

Lord, can I selfishly pray for a miracle? For Karoline to drop her guard long enough to see me?

Chapter Nineteen

♥

Mason - Present

KAROLINE WALKS BESIDE ME, talking about the movie as we trek a few blocks from the theater to someplace I may regret taking her. The cool night air is refreshing as we walk; it was a good decision to leave the truck parked at the theater.

"Mm, my favorite part was when the…" She animatedly describes a scene in the film where the female main character had to save the male main character from a trap he fell into because he didn't listen to the woman's advice. Of course that's the scene that stands out to her; who cares about the scene where the guy confessed his feelings to the woman and she willingly accepted him?

Not Karoline. Because that would be way too easy for her to do.

The woman is making me work for her, but honestly, when I think about it, I don't think I'd have it any other way. Karoline deserves to be pursued, and she certainly deserves to have someone prove themselves to her.

Hopefully what I have planned for tonight will help her see just how far I'm willing to go to earn her commitment.

"Mason?"

My name on her tongue never gets old. I stop, giving her my full attention. She sparkles under the moonlight as the stars dance in the sky, and suddenly, lyrics begin to form. A counter ballad to "Midnight Mistakes" takes root. "Hm?"

"Are we almost there? I'm starving. It's 10:30 p.m." Karoline brings one hand to her stomach while the other fiddles with her hair.

I point to a yellow-lit sign across the street and say a silent prayer that my plan goes accordingly. "Yep. Right there."

We both swallow at the same time as we stare at the diner in the distance. Now, I know what you're thinking. Finley the Wise told me not to take Karoline to diners because it would rehash the past. But that is my intention tonight… I want to show her what *should have* happened three years ago. I want to give her new memories to cling to.

"A… diner?" The tremble of her voice is like a guitar string snapping and popping me in the face.

God, please… Help me get this right.

"If you're uncomfortable, we can go elsewhere. I just… I figured we should face our past in some semblance since we can't go to Dallas Junction right now." I mean, we could… but I doubt she'd be down for that.

She looks from me to the diner a few times before straightening her shoulders and closing her eyes. I study her face, noticing the worry lines in her forehead and the stout pull of her lips together. But then she nods and says, "You're right.

It's the last barrier to our friendship. But while we are there, we are only talking about the questions you have regarding the commercial shoot tomorrow, okay?"

Relief floods through me and I crack a smile. I try not to dwell too much on the way she said *friendship* because a win is a win. "Great. Let's go."

As we began to cross the street, headlights illuminate the world around me.

No, not headlights...

I step in front of Karoline as a few people begin shouting my name. "Karoline," I whisper over my shoulder. "Paparazzi are here. I'm going to shrug my coat off, and I want you to put it on and tuck your face down. There is a pair of glasses in the pocket. Put them on. Do you have a ponytail holder?"

"N-no," she stammers. She remains pressed against my back as I slide my jacket off and hand it to her behind my back.

After she tells me she has the coat and sunglasses on, I pull the ponytail holder from my own hair. "Here. Put your hair up in this. I promise I'll keep you hidden from the vultures."

The flashes and noises grow closer, but thankfully, they are only coming in front of me and not behind us. I spin around so that I am face to face with Karoline.

"You stay in front of me, tucked into my side. I don't care if they see me, but I don't want them equating the woman on my arm to you. If we announce ourselves as a couple one day, it will be on our terms. Not theirs."

We begin walking, but Karoline is steadily tripping over her feet in her cloaked haste. "What do you mean by announcing ourselves as a couple? Mason! We are not a couple!"

"Not yet." I smirk, though I doubt she can see me by the way she is doing an accurate impression of the Hunchback of Notre Dame at the moment.

"Do you not understand what I said to you back at the theater? Did you not catch the word friendship a moment ago?"

"I understand everything, Karoline, except for why you continue to fight the feelings you have for me when I've shown you that I am all for you and only you over the past few weeks. And I'm sorry that I'm not just going to cave and walk away when the love of my life is worth fighting for."

When Karoline stumbles again, grabbing my arm to steady herself, I sigh. "Just remember that what I'm about to do is for your own good. You're a hazard unto yourself right now trying to outrun the paparazzi in your nervous condition. Come here."

I pick her up and toss her over my shoulder, careful to hold her dress down over her thighs. Now the paparazzi definitely won't see her face, and well, I'll have some interesting rumors circulating about me in about an hour.

Like the Princess Fiona character I know her to be, she bangs on my back like I'm Shrek, all the while yelling, "Put me down, you insufferable man!"

A chuckle escapes me, and I tap her bottom.

She stills, and then roars, "Mason Jonathan Kane! Did you just touch my butt?"

K AROLINE

"A tap for a slap. Are you done beating my back or do I need to give you a little love nudge again?" Mason has the audacity to continue laughing as I bounce up and down on his shoulder, the flashing cameras still illuminating our way back to his truck in the theater parking lot.

I'm wrapped in his jacket, which smells a lot like bad decisions and retribution. Okay, actually it's a musky scent that reminds me of the morning dew of a woodsy forest, but basically the same thing.

Because the fact that I haven't fought my way off this man's shoulder is indeed a deliciously wrong choice.

Sure, I banged on his back, but that was mainly to feel the muscles underneath the thin layer of shirt. If I truly wanted off, I would be off, and that is why I hate myself right now.

"No. No more love nudges or whatever you just called that monstrous action. Don't touch the butt…"

"Oh, but I like touching the butt…" The tease in his voice is a dangerous toxin meant to seduce me to his whims. No, sir. Not tonight.

"Then go swim with Nemo! This one is off limits."

He laughs again but respects my wishes. At my request, he turns me around to carry me bridal style so that his shoulder is no longer jamming into my stomach, and I don't think I want to ever leave his arms. I tuck my head into his chest and let the rhythm of his gait soothe my heightened nerves as the yelling and flashing chaos ensues behind us. His arms are my safe cocoon.

We reach his truck as the paparazzi swarm us. What started as a few ended up being at least ten, snapping pictures and hollering things at Mason like, "who's the girl" and "look at me" the entire time. He ignores them, taking special care to make sure I'm covered and shielded from their cameras.

At his careful and intentional actions, my heart swells with gratitude. It's not that I'm against the spotlight. If Mason and I *were* together—not that we will be or anything—I think I could handle it if he protected me like this. But I definitely don't want to be on the front page of a tabloid where I'd be labeled as Mason's fling or one-night-stand or whatever else they would come up with.

Maybe they are tracking us because Mason *is* with a girl... someone other than his friend Genevieve. From all my social stalking, Mason was never portrayed as a bad boy or player in the newspapers.

He may have dated around in high school and college, but the man in this truck with me now is not the one I used to know...

He cranks the truck and the engine roars, scattering the hive of busy bees who ruined my night with Mason. He peels out of the parking lot, leaving the group eating his dust. I silently cheer our victory and narrow escape.

"That was..."

"Fun," I finish as I meet his gaze. He smiles and shifts his eyes back to the road in front of us.

Silence surrounds us as we settle down from the rush of escaping the paparazzi.

Finally, I ask, "Is this what your life is like all the time? Constantly running from them?"

He shakes his head, causing his hair to whack him in the face. "Forgot I took the half-bun down." He chuckles, then continues. "No. Not really. I usually don't mind and have grown accustomed to never having a moment alone. That is, besides my time here in Mississippi."

A thoughtful expression crosses his face as he narrows his eyes. "I'm not sure how they found me, but I'm sorry you had to endure that. If they somehow got your picture and you end up unintentionally famous for a while, I'm very sorry, Vroom." His voice lowers as he concludes his sentence, letting me know he means what he's saying.

"Everything will be okay. I don't think they got a picture of me because I don't ever remember making eye contact with them. You protected me well." I smile at him and he practically beams back at me. "Even if... we grew up together. At the very least we can take control of the narrative by stating we are childhood friends reconnecting. We can tell the truth that you're helping me out by filming a commercial."

His hand slides down the steering wheel and rests in the open middle seat between us. I desperately want to grab it and weave my fingers between his, but I don't.

I can't.

Right?

"So much for bridging the last gap for our friendship," I dramatically sigh. "Guess we will have to forever remain on the outskirts since we couldn't go to the diner."

Mason glances my way with a raised, thick brow. "We can head to Dallas right now. Say the word." His voice tightens as we roll up to a stop sign and he pierces me with his eyes. "I would like to show you how that night three years ago should have gone."

The truck lurches forward. "What do you mean?"

Mason shrugs and under the street light, I notice a ghostly smile paints his face. "Another time."

Chapter Twenty

♥

Mason - Present

THE BOUTIQUE HAS BEEN transformed to a lovers' paradise of sorts. Between the hearts and the classic Valentine's Day colors of red, white, pink, and black, this place screams "season of love." Even a soft, feminine scent—something akin to a vanilla cupcake—infiltrates the air.

Even clothes on display are a contrast of Taylor Swift's Lover and Reputation.

Yes, I know Swift's music. What kind of musician would I be if I didn't know the most famous woman on the planet?

"Houston, we have a problem," Karoline says as I enter the employee area in the back. I look in her direction by the fold out table, and mercy... With the way she looks in those ripped skinny jeans and black long-sleeved baggy crop top, with her hair braided to one side, I'm almost to the point of dropping to my knees and begging for her affection. Yesterday, though it didn't go according to plan, was good for me and Karoline. After she made her feelings clear and I made my intentions known, we were able to look past the hurt for a moment to cut up and laugh. She even let me get away with flirting...

And that's a huge win in my book.

"What's wrong?" Hadley approaches, wearing a similar outfit to Karoline, though my Karoline rocks it better in my opinion. I suppose Braxton would say otherwise.

"Genevieve's manager just sent me a text telling me that Genevieve has the flu and can't make it to the filming. She, uh..." Karoline stammers, tugging at her braid, her eyes shifting from her phone, to Hadley, and then land on me. "She suggested that I take her place in the commercial."

My brain is throwing a party—confetti, cake, pointed paper hats, the whole nine yards. The script for the commercial is quite romantic, and it involves up-close and personal relations with the female lead. While I was comfortable performing the script with Gen, as she's a good friend, doing this with Karoline instead can only do one thing: help me continue to win her cold, hardened heart back to me.

"I'm fine with that," I pipe up. Both women stop the conversation they were having and swivel their heads to me. My manager, Rob, rolls his eyes from his position beside Hadley. I don't even hide the smile creeping up my face as I focus my attention on Karoline. "We have good chemistry. Better than the friendship type I have with Gen. Doing this with Karoline is the best option out there."

"And what do we tell the press when this is released and it basically verifies that you have a woman here in Mississippi? And everyone will connect the girl in the pictures to Karoline. With Gen, everyone knows the two of you are friends.

But the world now knows that you were with a woman last night, and it wasn't Genevieve Rhodes."

I shrug, still keeping my eyes locked on Karoline. To my thrill, she hasn't taken her gaze away from me. The images were online and circulating within an hour of our frenzied escape last night. I messaged Karoline to make sure she knew, and she called me and we sat on the phone scouring the internet to make sure her face never appeared. We got lucky. All the images and headlines reported I was secretly dating someone, but no one knew who.

That, my friend, is something I can live with. Go on and let the world think I have a girlfriend because, hopefully, it won't be a lie for much longer…

But for now…"We'll tell them the truth: Karoline and I are childhood friends." The sound of relieved breaths fills the silence around me, and I simply can't resist. "But I want so much more with her, and I plan to get it."

Rob chokes on something, probably his own spit. Hadley's smile resembles the Grinch's when he's plotting to steal Christmas, and Karoline's face flushes redder than the hearts hanging from the ceiling in this boutique.

"All right, I see you," Hadley says, walking a few steps over to me and patting me on the back. Then she turns to Karoline. "Let's get you ready for the camera."

While the ladies walk away, I send a quick text to Gen.

> **Me:** Idk if you're actually sick or not. If you are, I pray you get better soon. And if you're not… thank you.

She responds immediately.

> **Gen:** You're welcome *winky face*

K AROLINE

I'm a she-man.

As I look at myself in the floor-length mirror in our fitting rooms, I scowl at the hulkish woman staring back at me… and also the ridiculous heart cut-outs lining the mirror's edge. We always do way too much for holidays in this store, but this holiday is the worst. It's not even a real holiday, after all. It's just a beacon for singles to feel bad about themselves. Like me. Maybe that's why I'm low-key hating my body right now.

Because no one wants it.

Except maybe Mason…

NO. He's the one person who can't have it…

Right?

Someone tell me I'm right, please, because the way he got boyishly excited over filming this commercial with me earlier had me thinking that I could easily slip back into loving him.

Or at least continually consciously admitting to myself that I've always loved him…

"Hadley. Do I really have to wear this? I'm not built like Genevieve." I slide my clammy hands down the skin-tight strappy pink mini dress. Tassels hang off the bottom, swishing and caressing the bottom half of my exposed thighs and tops of my kneecaps. While I'm tall and lean like Genevieve, I definitely have more muscle definition and broader shoulders. I'm not necessarily a "soft" woman. And this Pepto-pink color is atrocious. It's too Valentine's Day, and that's NOT the look I'm going for.

Hadley looks me over in the mirror, a whole head shorter than me in these three-inch baby pink stiletto heels. "I think you look amazing, but I don't want you to be uncomfortable. Let's see what else we can…"

Eyeing my jeans and black crop I previously had on, I interrupt Hadley's tassel-fied train of thought. "Couldn't I just wear some clothes from our boutique? It would make sense to rep the boutique and the jewelry since the goal is to merge the brands together, right?"

"And this is why you are in charge of marketing." Hadley laughs. "But let's find the cutest, country-iest, trendiest thing we carry."

She slips out of the dressing room while I tug at this monstrosity of a dress. The tassels tangle in my wavy hair as I yank the dress off, and I wish I had kept my hair in its braid. After taking off the heels, I examine my frame, noting how much my body has changed in three years. Without that dress on, I'm quite proud of my body. I'm sharper, more refined, though my hips are more defined in contrast to my waist. It's amazing how much can change in three years…

Mason.

The thought of him on the other side of this dressing room causes my temperature to rise… but not in a hate-filled way.

I'm standing in my black bra and underwear, with the man I hate to love on the other side of this thick curtain. The man who has, admittedly, seemed to have changed the same way my body has over the past few years. Though he's still absolutely the natural flirt I know him to be, he's been nothing but sincere in his apologies to me. And, I think, sincere in his desire for me…

What if…

What if I let him back in? What if I accepted him? Lord knows I wanted to kiss Mason's face off in the theater last night, but I stopped myself because I'm still uncertain. The fear that he doesn't truly want me, and instead wants me because he can't have a different girl, is still clouding my judgment.

But he's Mason Kane. Girls are constantly throwing themselves at him. I've seen the fan-pages created for him…

Mason could have any woman he desired.

But he is actively pursuing me.

He really has changed, hasn't he?

I think back to that night three years ago. It still stings, but… it's not as bad as it once was.

Is that because of the time I've spent with Mason recently? Is it because he has been respectful of my wishes? Sure, he has flirted relentlessly, but I don't expect anything less than that. It's who he is: a sunshiney, happy-go-lucky flirt.

He's made his intentions clear. He said he wants me, and I...

I think I believe him.

"How about this?" Hadley pokes her head into the dressing room, and below the floating head is a hovering hand holding a bundle of clothes.

"Just get in here." I wave her in. The curtains open enough to let her through, but even in that little opening, I lock eyes with Mason, and immediately throw myself against the back corner to shield my body. Within seconds, the curtain is shut tightly and Hadley is unfolding clothes.

But my chest is heaving, and my brain conjures scenarios where Hadley is not present and Mason rips open the curtain to claim me with his lips, and...

NO! Jeez, Karoline. Collect yourself. Just because you're ovulating does not give you permission to fantasize about Mason. Or any man for that matter. Clean thoughts only...

"Okay, put this on." Hadley, bless her, interrupts my thoughts, thrusting clothes in my direction.

No. Not thrusting. Handing me clothes. Just handing me...

Oh, God. Please help me to redirect my thoughts.

Repeating my silent prayer mantra, I throw on the clothes Hadley brought in, finally opting for a simple black dress with a lace trim that, to me, screams "I hate Valentine's Day" in the most subtle way.

Chapter Twenty-One

♥

Karoline - Present

MASON'S COOL, MINTY BREATH washes over the back of my neck, sending waves of chills rippling down my spine. His calloused fingertips brush my collar bone as he traces the silver necklace he just clasped to my neck.

Something between a sigh and a moan escapes unbidden between my parted lips, and I close my eyes, leaning my head back and onto Mason's strong, sturdy shoulders. My back is pressed up against him in all the right ways, and I think about that day out at the lake a few years ago…

"Cut!" the director yells, snapping me back to reality like I'm Slim Shady.

I shake the fog from my head and lurch away from Mason, but his finger is apparently still hitched on the necklace, and the forward momentum causes the silver cord of the necklace to clothesline against my windpipes, effectively cutting my breath off and creating a lingering feeling that I'm suffocating.

And then the pressure releases and I tumble forward, crashing down on my knees.

"Oh, crap," Mason hollers then appears in front of me in a squatted position, reaching out towards my face. He stops at the last second and his hand drops, stirring a sudden desire to feel his calloused fingertips on my cheek. "Are you okay? I didn't mean to let go and make you fall, but you were choking."

I hold up a hand and speak through gasps as I catch my breath. "I'm okay. Just give me a minute."

I'm really fine. The whole shebang took less than five seconds, but I need to pretend to recoup simply due to the embarrassment flooding my system. Everyone—the cameraman, Hadley, the lighting and sound people, Rob—just witnessed me losing myself in Mason and then getting choked out by a freaking necklace...

Is that thing made of steel or something? How did it not snap? I suppose that could be a selling point?

Or something we should sweep under the rug and never mention to a single soul. If humans with murderous, foul intentions ever found this out...

I push myself to my feet; Mason scoops his hands underneath my elbows to assist me. I run my hands down the black midi dress and check to make sure the lace bottom is intact. It is, and thankfully, so are my knees, with the exception of the bruises that I know will mark both of them come tomorrow.

"You could use that necklace to kill a man," I joke with Hadley, who places one hand on a hip and narrows her eyes at me.

"I will not have my jewelry be associated with murder."
She looks around. "Oh, Mr. Hanes," she addresses the cameraman, "could you so kindly make sure there is no footage
of my necklace choking out my employee?"

"Yes," Rob chimes in. "And I can't have footage of Mason
being the one initiating the choking."

Mason and I exchange glances, then we burst out laughing
as we watch our people harass the poor cameraman, both of
them looking over his shoulders at the footage he caught.

"That is my type of Valentine's Day commercial." Mason
says, his laughter dying off. "Murderous necklaces and you
in a black dress."

A blush coats my cheeks as he doubles down on his comment by trailing his eyes over me. Sweat prickles at the
edges of my neck from the heat of his gaze. I attempt to
change the subject. "Well, black is technically a color that's
associated with Valentine's Day, you know, because of the
sensual aspect of the color…" Dang it. The subject change
is not going well for me. He raises his brow as he crosses
his arms and cocks his hip, not bothering to hide his smirk
while I clear my throat. "But in my opinion, it symbolizes
rebelling against the ridiculous made-up holiday."

He rolls his eyes and drops his hands to his sides. "Aw,
come on, Vroom. It's not a bad holiday. The decorations can
be," he glances around the room, "excessive. But it's about
celebrating something special. Love."

"Love is for the birds."

"Love is for everyone. It's a beautiful gift given to us by the One who is the embodiment of love... Jesus Christ. We can love because He loves us."

I'm speechless at his words. My mind attempts to reconcile the man I knew three years ago who would go to church only when it was convenient for him. While Mason and I have not had a faith conversation of our own, I do know that he is a believer now. That's one thing Mom has made clear to me every time I've talked to her about this job I'm doing with Mason. *He's changed. He's different. He follows the Lord.*

And by the sincerity of his statement and the joy radiating in his eyes...

Mom was right.

Oh, Lord...

My heart explodes without my consent, and just like that, I know I'm a complete goner for this man in front of me. A man who will truly know how to love me because he has experienced the true source of love...

Mason steps in my direction; his hand flexes at his side as if he is going to reach for me, but he doesn't.

And once again, I'm immensely disappointed.

So I reach for him and all laughter ceases.

I want this man more than I have ever desired anything in my life...

Can I truly have him? Can he be mine?

My hand cups his cheek, then my fingers slide into his thick, chocolate hair. "Mason..."

His name is a whispered plea on my lips.

Mason, please don't hurt me.

Mason, please don't break my heart.

Mason, please don't run away.

Mason, please love me the way I love you…

His large hand covers mine, and he places his other on the small of my back, tugging me close so that I'm forced to tilt my head to meet his warm, smoldering eyes.

Yes, smoldering. I've always wondered what it would be like to have Mason look at me like this.

It's burning me alive. Like I'm standing a little too close to the sun.

"Mason…" His name escapes my lips once more.

He pulls me flush against him and into a tight hug. My hands drop around his neck as if it's the most natural action in the world.

Mason's lips linger near my ear, his breath tickling my skin. "Karoline, I know you are scared. You have every right to doubt me. But please, you have to see how special and important you are to me. You have to know I came back for you. These past three years of my life have been great but something was missing. You. You are the missing piece in my life. Every song I wrote while away from you contains traces of us."

His words are like lightning strikes to my once-stopped heart. He is resurrecting every feeling and dream I had buried six feet under because I believed it was a lost cause. People make mistakes, even big ones. But that doesn't mean we stay there. Mason has proven he has changed. His reputation is clean. He doesn't drink anymore. He's doing what I wanted him to do years ago, which is to actively pursue me. He is sorry. And I…

I believe him.

Pulling away and meeting his hungry eyes, I stand on my tiptoes and tilt my head as his lips twitch into a smile. He closes his eyes…

"Okay, everyone. Let's try to shoot from this angle now." The director's voice cuts through the moment, and I shake my head and open my eyes. Mason mimics my expression—bright eyes, a hint of sadness that the moment is gone by the slight frown he wears, but there's something else there…

His frown turns into a smirk as his gaze burns on my lips. "One second, Camera Man."

My eyebrows knit and I tilt my head to the side. "Mason, you have to let me go so we can finish this commercial."

He laughs, a miraculous sound as if he just discovered a treasure chest or something. Mason whispers as his head lowers towards mine. "Nah. I'm not letting you go. In fact, I'm going to kiss you, Vroom."

And like in the movies, the world in fact fades away as I give in to what I've always known to be true, even if the clueless man in front of me was late to the game. Mason and I were meant to be.

End of story.

"I dare you, Peppermint," I breathe against the soft touch of his lips.

His mouth moves slowly against mine; an explosion of pent-up feelings spew out of me like I'm an erupting volcano and he is the earthquake that triggered it. All the years I've spent enclosing the love I have for him with boards of hate and nails of fault fade away. I'm left with raw love and a grateful heart for the path that got us to this moment. The Mason of three years ago was not what I needed, but this Mason is. He's sure, steady, and level-headed without losing his sense of humor and flirty nature. And his faults, which seem to primarily lay in his lack of patience, are not deal breakers to me.

And this is what our first kiss should have been like. What it should have tasted like...

Peppermint coats my tongue. My arms move to wrap around his neck while his other hand joins the one already pressed against my back. I joyfully press my body flat against his as he deepens the kiss with a low, rumbly groan.

We stand there, working in tandem to show each other just how much we mean to one another, soaking in each other as the world disappears around us. Three years was worth the wait. This version of Mason is everything I wanted and so much more.

A throat clears, and I release Mason from the jail cell that is my arms, though Mason does not let me out of his grip. We are breathing heavily, and I'm positive I'm wearing the same expression as him: fire burning in half-moon eyes that scream desire for so much more...

"Okay, let's begin the next shoot, please," the director calls again, clearly uncomfortable with PDA. I can't blame him. It's not for everyone...

Looks like the two of us don't mind, however.

The corner of Mason's lips twitches before he drops one hand from my back. He weaves his fingers through mine and gently squeezes as he pulls me impossibly closer, his fingers splaying across my lower back.

For the rest of eternity, there will be a Mason-sized hand-print seared into my back.

"Let's get this over with so that I can take you on a real date tonight, Karoline Renee Wright. One that we both view as a date. To the diner because I want to show you just what I should have done when you confessed to me three years ago. And I will warn you, it involves many sober kisses and innocent touches and me adoring you like you deserve to be adored. Be prepared, *Little Ma'am*."

His use of my full name sends butterflies fluttering in my stomach, not to mention his straightforward intentions. And heaven help me, I can't wait!

"Sounds like a plan," I say, though my voice comes out hoarse, like I'm in desperate need of a gallon of water. I clear my throat. "Sorry. Yes, I'd like that very much."

Mason walks us the short distance to where the camera man needs us for the next part of the shoot. I sneak a glance at Hadley, who is giving me two thumbs up. She then proceeds to make kissy faces, and I roll my eyes.

But I also smile.

I'm scared senseless, but this is Mason.

His favorite color is olive green. His favorite song is "I Walk the Line" by Johnny Cash. His favorite food is a medium rare steak with a big helping of mashed potatoes. He's a flirt with a huge heart, and though a total ladies' man, he is loyal to a fault. Not once over our years together did he ever cheat on a woman; in fact, he was the one mostly dumped.

Mason is kind, generous, and cares too much for his own good. He donates to a variety of charities, he is always interacting with his fans, even when he's exhausted and tired after a show, and he is intentional with every move he makes.

Though I haven't been around Mason in three years, my social-stalking has paid off. It's like we never skipped a beat.

Mason *has* changed, and not once have I read an article where he got drunk or was caught drinking with friends or had wild nights with women.

His reputation has been spotless.

Mason Jonathan Kane is sincere.

The boy who left me three years ago is no longer in existence; in his place is a sure and steady, hardworking, dime of a man.

And I'm cashing in on him.

Chapter Twenty-Two

Mason - One Year Ago

"I 'M GOING TO BUILD a home here."

"There's no way," Rob says, pacing a hole on the stage that's in the process of being taken down. The summer heat is oppressing, much like my mood at the moment. Last night's show here in Biloxi was a huge success, but that's not why I want to move to Mississippi.

I saw her.

Karoline.

She was looking gorgeous in a pink tassel dress and boots. Her hair was curled. I don't know how I spotted her amidst the crowd, but there she was, like a beacon calling me home.

She left during "Midnight Mistakes," the very song I wrote about her, and there was nothing I could do about it.

I wanted to stop the song, call her name, and tell her to meet me backstage. Who cares about a concert when the love of your life, the woman who ruined you for all other women, is only a floor-crowd away from you?

But I have a career to uphold and there's a better way of reconciling with her than stopping a concert.

"Yes. I am. And there's nothing you can do to stop me. I'll wait until this tour is over, but when it is, I'm heading to Juniper Grove."

Rob curses. "Mason, why? What does that little, no-name town have to offer you? We need to stay in Nashville."

"Karoline. It has Karoline to offer, and that's a better offer than anything Nashville can give me." I sigh, rubbing a hand through my tousled hair. It is still sticky with sweat from the concert tonight. Lyrics drift through my mind, a little ditty about chasing the woman you love to the ends of the earth to prove your love to her. "Look. I'm not quitting music. I'm not giving up this career. I just… I need her. And even if I can't have her because of what I did to her, I need to make it right. Somehow, someway. I have to try. It's been too long, and I have to man up and face her. I love her, and I want the chance to finally apologize and earn her trust and eventually love. She's the woman for me, Rob."

Rob stares at me, mouth agape. "What did you do to that poor girl?"

I breathe a mirthless laugh. "Nothing good. But I'm determined to make it right, and to do that, I need to be in Juniper Grove for a while."

"Okay, Mason. Whatever you say. As long as you don't up and leave me."

I chuckle. "My days of up and leaving people are over. Don't worry. Now, let's help with getting this stuff taken down. I'm ready for bed."

Chapter Twenty-Three

♥

Karoline - Present

"THANK YOU FOR COMING out tonight to our Valentine's Day West Coast Swing Celebration," the young, sandy-blond male serving as tonight's announcer says, spreading his arms out like an eagle's wings. Like everyone else, he's dressed in casual but trendy clothes, perfect for dancing but not the typical outdated swing outfits.

Mason squeezes my hand, and I stare lovingly at my boyfriend. We've been dating for about a month, and his vacation home was finished a couple of weeks ago. It surprised me that he stuck around; he is scheduled to release another album in March. He has been driving back and forth from here to Nashville every week despite my protest that he should simply stay in Nashville until the launch of his album since I worked a lot and had school anyways. He said that was not an option, and well, I didn't complain.

The announcer continues. "We've been blessed to teach the Juniper Grove area and surrounding cities the beauty of swing dancing for the past twenty-five years. Tonight's community event is hosted by me, Stone Harper, director of The Grove Community Center. While we provide a place for teens to hang out and interact face-to-face in a safe environment on the daily, we also host community events once a month. The West Coast Swing Company was gracious in allowing us to use their facility for tonight's Valentine's Day improv event. I also want to thank my assistant and stand-in event coordinator, Lucy Spence, for making this happen for us tonight." He gestures to Lucy who is smiling and waving in her black tights, pink, cropped tank top dotted with little white hearts, and black canvas ballroom shoes. Her Ariana Grande-style high strawberry blonde ponytail swings as she attempts to meet every gaze in the room. The woman is a natural when it comes to being in the spotlight.

"Lucy will tell you all the rules of conduct for the night, then we'll call out the numbers for the first random coupling for the first improv of the night." He meets our gazes and grins. "Actually, we should let our special guest, country artist Mason Kane, go first. What do y'all say?"

The large room erupts in shouts and applause, the sound waves bouncing off the hallowed walls and sleek hardwood floor. Red, pink, black, and white hues swirl around the room like a wildfire as participants swing a variety of square pillows in circles over their heads. Hadley, Braxton, Lorelei, Chanel, Malik, and I join in on the stimulating chaos of the crowd while Mason stands and waves to everyone.

Lucy grabs the mic from Stone as the crowd dies down. "All right, y'all. Let's get this night started. A few rules to remember…"

As Lucy talks, something akin to a thrilling version of anxiety floods my system. It's been three years since I last danced West Coast Swing... and it was with the man standing beside me on the side of the dance floor. It was the night after I graduated; Mason surprised me with a graduation party at the local dance company we frequented. It was a pleasurable night of line dancing, swing dancing, and even the occasional country-fied salsa... the best way to celebrate, in my opinion. Especially because Mason danced with me most of the night, only allowing others to step in a handful of times.

"Come on up, Mason!" the announcer shouts to a roar of claps by all and hopeful shouts given by a group of young females on the other side of the room. I resist the urge to scowl in their direction.

How can they be so "in your face" when his girlfriend is in the room?

And yes, all of the nation knows I am Mason Kane's girlfriend. When that commercial aired a week ago, we also came clean about our relationship. While the majority of comments on our social media—I've gained thousands upon thousands of followers simply because I'm his girl—have been kind and supportive, there are those who are not happy that their celebrity man-crush is taken.

Mason stands by the announcer—Stone, if I recall correctly—and waves with a big grin to the crowd still cheering him on.

"Have you ever danced West Coast Swing?" Stone asks.

Mason locks eyes with me, and I want to jump up and kiss him senseless in front of everyone. We shared our first *real* kiss in front of people; he and I quickly discovered that we are *that* PDA couple.

"Yes. In fact, I took lessons throughout high school with my lover."

All eyes turn to me, and I sheepishly wave. *Lover? Where did that come from…* Yes, we've said our I love yous, because well, we've meant those words longer than the two of us have known, but still. Wouldn't the title of girlfriend be sufficient?

Emotional men… what will we ever do with them?

Heh. I'm going to love the mess out of mine.

"Well, I know this is supposed to be random, but why don't the two of you kick off tonight's shindig?"

Lucy begins a chant that spreads throughout the room. "Do it. Do it. Do it!"

Hadley stands then yanks me to my feet. I nod my head to the crowd and walk towards my man, who is currently the only thing keeping me from puking because of the nerves. I'm wearing an anxious smile alongside my black dance shoes, black leggings with silver swirl designs, and red halter-style sports bra—forever sporting my favorite brand from my favorite boutique, which has become a national icon, alongside Tease Jewelry, for all us middle-class girlies in the span of the week. The yawn that escapes me as I stand in front of everyone has everything to do with working late hours and trying to keep up with my school work.

"Someone had a long night with her beau," Stone wiggles his eyebrows just as Lucy slaps him on the forearm.

My face heats, but Mason is quick on his feet. "Nah. It's not me. My woman here is a hard-working marketing specialist." He grabs my hand and then leads us to the center of the dance floor. "Let's get this night started. What will we be dancing to?"

The DJ in the corner whispers in Stone's ear, and he perks up. "Let's find out!"

Music blares through the sound system, a country twang that at first, I suspect to be one of Mason's songs. But, it's not, and as Chris Stapleton's new song, "I Think I'm in Love with You," plays, Mason begins to lead me in a sensual swing dance that has the audience going feral.

Much like me at the moment...

The way Mason moves against me, my word.

Our dancing chemistry is very much intact from years ago, but this... It's the grown-up version of what we used to do. Mason doesn't shy away from hand placement. His hands touch me...

All. Over.

He dips me and tugs me close. He spins me and gives me room to do little quirky, albeit sexy, moves that the audience eats up. No doubt this dance will be all over social media soon.

The song lyrics dictate and guide us, a song we are both familiar with because it perfectly describes our situation: a man who was ignorant to his feelings towards a woman in the past but now has blissfully accepted them and pursued her.

As we dance, Mason leans in and whispers, "You should wear that pink tasseled dress you wore to my concert in Biloxi last year. Imagine swing dancing in that. I almost stopped the entire show for you that night, Vroom."

Last month's version of me would have died of embarrassment at being caught in one of the most conflicting, emotional moments of my life. A moment that I view as my lowest in my desperate pursuit to get over him.

But now…?

I lean in and press my lips against his ear as our bodies sway to the ending music. "I still have it. Tucked away in the back of my closet. I'll wear it just for you, Peppermint. To your next concert. Where I'll be standing in the wings waiting to kiss you senseless after the show."

He doesn't blush, nor does he gawk at my boldness. Instead, he manages to pull me closer against him and kisses *me* senseless as the song comes to an end.

This is us. The real version of who we are together. Unashamed. Confident.

In love.

The crowd is chunking pillows at us left and right, and when we break apart, we both wave at the crowd and take little bows. We take our seat back on the floor with our friends, and Stone goes on and on about how it would be nearly impossible to beat our performance tonight.

"And the next contestant is…" He draws a name from the bowl. "Oh, wow. It's me! How did my name get in here?"

We all chuckle at his genuinely shocked expression. The DJ in the corner points to himself, eliciting more laughter from the audience.

Lucy plunges her hand into the female name bowl. "And Stone's partner will be…"

She plucks a name, not unlike Effie Trinket from *The Hunger Games.* Her smile drops and she scans the crowd. "Who put my name in here?"

Beside me, Hadley points to Lorelei, who simply shrugs.

"No, I can't do this. Let me draw…"

Stone interrupts over the mic. "Rules are rules, Lucy May." He holds out a hand. "Shall we dance, my lady?"

Lucy is moving the mic from her face as she grimaces at Stone's hand, but it still catches her saying, "Never in a million years."

Stone sets his mic on the table behind him and clutches Lucy's hand, who drops her mic, the feedback causing everyone to cover their ears. Stone bends down and picks up the mic then sets it beside his. As he continues to hold on to Lucy's hand, he basically has to drag her kicking and screaming to the center of the floor.

He grabs her forearms and centers her when she tries to dash away, and then he whispers something in her ear, causing her already reddened face to deepen into a maroon color.

Poor girl.

I get the feeling this man is into her…

And by the looks of him, a natural flirt like my Mason, her romantic heart doesn't stand a fighting chance.

Unless Prince Finley Andersson sweeps her off her feet first.

Personally, I'm rooting for those two.

THE NIGHT FINALLY COMES to a close. Mason and I each danced one more time at random, and though we danced well, it was nothing like when the two of us danced together.

In fact, we did win the night. Got flowers and crowns to prove it.

As we are assisting with clean up—a *marvelous* benefit of knowing one of the hosts—Mason continuously tugs me off into shadowed corners to kiss me. Once everything is packed up and the building cleaned, we all head over to grab a late rooftop dinner at Lake View, courtesy of my very rich boyfriend.

We arrive and are ushered up to the roof. My jaw drops when I walk through the doors and see my parents and Mason's, already sitting at a table that's been set with white cloth and daisy center pieces. The chaos of the New Years Eve party hosted here has been long cleaned, but now, there's a new chaos happening as rose petals line the floor and swirl in the light breeze on occasion. It's romantic as heck, and perfect for this holiday I once swore to loathe.

After taking in the scene, I run to hug my mama and dad before turning to greet his parents.

"What are y'all doing here?" I ask.

"We just missed our kids," Mama says. "And now that the two of you finally came to your senses and got together, we wanted to check in and see how everything was going."

"Everything is great." Mason grins, slipping an arm behind my back. I stare at him with stars in my eyes. He doesn't look surprised at all. In fact, he looks... pleased?

I frown. "What's really going on here?" His parents shrug with a knowing smile.

Mason laughs and leads me to stand at the edge of the rooftop. We both stare out across the way; the stars shine brightly across an endless night sky... as endless as my love for the man beside me. Whatever is going on, I trust Mason. Something I once thought I'd never be able to say.

"I have a little surprise for you," he says. Then he walks a short distance to grab his guitar case (not sure how that got here as it wasn't with him when we arrived).

He pulls out that cherry-red guitar I saw him with when I went to his concert as an act of torture upon myself. The memory doesn't sting anymore. Instead, it serves as a reminder of how I've always loved Mason. I just masked the love in layers upon layers of hate because of how he hurt me.

But that's all in the past.

Mason strums the guitar, and after getting the right tune, he turns his beautiful eyes upon me and begins to play a song that sounds eerily like "Midnight Mistakes" but different...

Joyful? He holds my gaze as he begins to sing the most perfect acoustic country ballad I've ever heard.

"Dancing stars
Full moon of possibilities
You're here in my arms again
This night can never end
Tell me you'll stay
Forever my saving grace
Karoline Renee
Will you take my last name?"

My heart explodes with happiness as Mason, who had been walking towards me with every line of the song, sets his guitar down and takes a knee. "It's not finished, but it's your song. Karoline Renee Wright. Vroom." He smirks. "*Little Ma'am.* Happy Valentine's Day."

Every molecule of my being comes alive seeing him down on one knee in front of me. My heart pounds beneath my rib cage, and my hands start to sweat despite the cool night breeze.

Maybe this holiday isn't so bad after all…

Mason pulls out a small, black box and opens it. A beautiful but simple ring with a golden band and a diamond sits in the box, waiting to be put onto my finger. Mason continues, "I know I'm in love with you, and I have been for a very long time. I was too young and naïve to know it three years ago when I should have, but I know it now. And I don't want to waste another minute of this life not having you by my side at every turn. Karoline, will you be my designated valentine forever—will you marry me?"

I nod my head, salty tears streaming down my face. He stands, and I jump into his arms, wrap my legs around his waist, and kiss my fiancé.

His lips are warm against mine as he holds me close against him. I silently pray as we kiss, thankful for our painful journey and where it brought us.

When he sets me down, he slips the ring onto my finger, and we turn around and hold up my hand for our friends and family to see. They are clapping and hollering and popping sparkling water (because I will never touch alcohol again due to supporting my soon-to-be husband's sobriety).

Mason wraps me in his arms again and whispers against my ear, "I love you so much, Vroom. I'm sorry it took me so long to realize it."

I smile then pull back to look into his warm eyes that will forever be my home. "I forgive you. Who knows what would have happened if we hadn't taken the course that we did?"

"Wise words, my love."

I quickly kiss him. "Hm. 'My love.' I think you'll have to use that from now on."

"Not a chance. You'll always be my Vroom."

I finger the tattoo on my neck. "And you'll always be my Peppermint. Think we could get a speedy car tattooed on you?"

He laughs as he draws me in for another kiss. "Your name is already tattooed on my heart, so why not?"

When I slip my phone from my pocket, I notice I missed a text from him earlier while we were at the community center.

> **Peppermint:** You're talking with Lorelei and laughing, and I can't stop thinking about how beautiful you are. Just you wait for tonight...

"Ah, I see you've finally upgraded my name." Mason laughs, and I shove playfully into his side.

"Contact names are important. But I promise, this will forever be your name in my phone."

"Deal," Mason says, swooping in to steal a kiss.

"Happy Valentine's Day," I whisper against his soft lips.

Acknowledgments

This book wasn't supposed to exist. At least, not in this capacity. I had ideas for Karoline and Mason, but I never intended it to be a Valentine's Day book. Nor did I intend for the theme of constant, unwavering pursuit to present itself. But as a writer, my own life and experiences get in the way, and writing this book was like applying balm to my wounded heart. I wrote TDV in one month, and now, I wouldn't have this story take place any other way.

Thank you to my Lord and Savior Jesus Christ for the gift of writing. It took me a while to finally say "yes" to the call, but now I can't imagine doing anything else. I love teaching, but writing is my heart. *Soli Deo Gloria.*

To my family—Mama, Dad, Turan, Jace, and Grandma—thanks for always cheering me on and supporting me. My sweet besties—Callie, Kaitlyn, Aubrey, Whitney, and Abby. I love you ladies so much! Thanks for always being a listening ear.

To all my IG/Bookish friends…y'all are the literal best. The #bookstagram community is a light in a dark world. I'm so thankful for all the new author and reader friends I have because of that platform. Who says some of your closest friends can't be online?!

A special thank you to Leah Taylor who is the World's Greatest Editor. Seriously, she's not only an amazing editor, but also an amazing human and friend. I'm thankful she's in my corner. Callie, again... she's the World's Greatest Cartoon Character Artist in my opinion!

To my launch team, betas, and arc readers... THANK YOU. I could not be an indie author without your constant love, support, and excitement! You keep me going. To my readers... What more can I say? I sure can't say thank you enough. A writer is nothing without a reader. You are the lifeline of this career. This book belongs to you now.

Lastly, as the dedication states, to all the girls who have loved or currently love a man who just doesn't get the memo that he should pursue you as Christ pursues us... I pray you find a strong, God-fearing man who will! He's rare, but he's out there, ladies.

Also By

Drew Taylor

The Politics of… series (sweet romance)
The Politics of Christmas (#1)
The Politics of Love (#2)
The Politics of Ikigai (#3) **Coming 2025**

Designated series (sweet romantic comedy)
The Designated Friend (#1)
The Designated Valentine (#1.5)
The Designated Twin (#2) **Coming June 2024**
The Designated Date (#3) **Coming 2025**

About Author

Drew loves to write clean stories that leave you swooning and yearning for more. She believes romance isn't just about the physical, but about connections, friendships, and commitment. She is here to tell you that romance with Christian characters/themes can be hilarious, witty, and swoon-worthy.

Drew is from south Mississippi, where her heart lies, but now resides in Alaska where she teaches English. When not teaching or writing, she enjoys reading, Bookstagram, baking, researching random history facts, and spending time with her family and friends.

Follow Drew on Instagram and Facebook: @authordrewtaylor

Bonus Material

"Boyfriend Without Benefits"
Mason Kane

Verse 1:
It's late, awe, but honey I don't care
You text, me, and baby I'm right there
Dressed to the nines in a suit and tie
Or ripped up jeans and boots and a smile
Your hands, wrapped, around my arm
A kiss, on, the cheek so warm
Waving at your friends like I'm the one
Then toss me to the curb when the night is done

Refrain:
I'll never know just what you're thinking
So lately I've just been drinking
Cause...

Chorus:
I'm just a boyfriend without the benefits
your favorite arm candy without sweet kisses.
But I'll come runnin' every time you call

'cause no matter how deep I fall
I'll stay by your side
with wounded pride
as your boyfriend…

without the benefits.

Verse 2:
Bowling, movies, clubbing all night
The farm, riding, horses so right
Flaunt me all around this stoplight town
I'll never say no 'cause you're my sound

Refrain:
I'll never know just what you're thinking
So lately I've just been drinking

Chorus:
I'm just a boyfriend without the benefits
your favorite arm candy without sweet kisses.
But I'll come runnin' every time you call
'cause no matter how deep I fall
I'll stay by your side
with wounded pride
as your boyfriend…
without the benefits.

Refrain:
Baby tell me what you're thinking
'Cause I'm tired of all this drinking
Wishing I was more than just a…

Chorus:
Boyfriend without the benefits
your favorite arm candy without sweet kisses.
But I'll come runnin' every time you call
'cause no matter how deep I fall
I'll stay by your side
with wounded pride
as your boyfriend…
without the benefits.

Printed in Great Britain
by Amazon